HEART'S VOW

Mafia Brides Book 1

ROGUE LONDON

Red Hot Romance Inc

ACKNOWLEDGMENTS

They say it takes a town to raise a child. For an author, it takes a community of talented individuals. In my case, I have a tribe that helps me, and without them, getting my work out there would be a nightmare.

My publishing family at Red Hot Romance, Maren Smith, Rayanna Jamison, Maggie Ryan, Robin Smith, Stella Moore, and Allysa Hart. You are the best and I'm so grateful to get to work with you all.

Deborah Apodaca, an amazing woman that I'm so blessed to have in my life. I first met Deb when I wrote my Angels and Demons Series as Skylar West. She gave me wonderful reviews, so naturally, I reached out to her. We became fast friends, and the rest is history.

My writing bestie, Ann Jensen, with whom I write a sexy hot Masters of Midgard series. She invested hours of her time helping me layout and shape this new series and is always there to help me smooth out my rough edges and remind me who I am.

Skylar, not my alter ego, but my youngest child who is a huge supporter of me and my work and helps me creatively.

My Street Team... Cathleen Sarna (Cat), Imari McClure, and Dorothy Nunamacher, Alexis Lopez-McNelis for not only reading and sharing their thoughts on my work but also promoting and sharing on their social media. I have a special lady, Nicole Austin, who is my number one cheerleader and always brightens my day when I get down. She sends books to my team for me and helps my wonderful PA Deborah with contests.

And lastly and far from the least, my amazing ARC team who reads my work and shares their reviews with the world.

Thank you all! xo

HEART'S VOW PLAYLIST

https://open.spotify.com/playlist/3xRbnP2dor4L1M7CNjaF1C?
si=c2cfd477614b43f3&fbclid=IwAR3Bs2JsmskwvKietuHlFbDa5KRhpoPuZm-
j5aDkWZcymAWu2D7ekWxB3rs&nd=1

Castle by Halsey
Dirty Thoughts by Chloe Adams
You Don't Own Me by Joan Jett
Before you go by Lewis Capaldi
Heart Attack by Demi Lovato
Boss by Tony Effe
Control by Halsey
Monster by Skillet
Pain Three Days Grace
Cage the Beast Adelitas Way
Give your heart a break by Demi Lovato
The Monster by Eminem & Rhianna
Part Goddess part Gangster by Madalen Duke
Destroyer Of Monsters and Men
Freak but When it ends its not streets Midnightdrives
No Regrets by Wayne Murray, Timothy Fleet, Lana McDonagh

CHAPTER ONE

Romeo

Beside me, Massimo, my best friend and *consigliere* stood as still as a statue. The only giveaway that he was on high alert was his eyes, which constantly roved through the room, taking in every detail and assessing every potential threat. Lined up at his side, stood our five brothers. Not that we were all related by blood. My father brought Massimo and his two brothers, Antonio and Gaetano, to live with us after their parents died, taken out by a warring mob.

That was a long time ago, before my youngest blood-brother, Vincenzo, was born, completing our family. Even as my mother held Vinny in her arms while we crowded around to see the newest member of the family, I could sense the bond between us all, and I was not the only one. "Lucky number seven," my father proclaimed proudly. "A band of brothers!"

This nickname for our family tribe became a title of fear in the larger *la familia,* of which the Vitales were in the top tier. We were lucky in our education by my father, who never mistreated us and allowed our roles within the family dynamic to organically happen. My brothers and I were raised with love and respect by both our parents, and no one would dare question our toughness, as we were the undisputed heirs to my father's kingdom, with a role to play within the family.

Now I stood on the precipice of matrimonial bliss, the first of us to take a wife. Bliss was doubtful, as this was a business arrangement and experience had showed me that marriages within the mafia were based on roles, not love and happiness. I didn't expect home-cooked meals or terms of endearment from my new wife, only that she perform her duties as Mrs. Vitale. Obedience was key in my world as it could be the difference between life and death. Failure on Vittoria's part to fall in line would earn her punishments over my knee as I seared the lesson into her flesh with my hand.

Somehow, I doubted she would be a willing participant and would have to learn the hard way. Her father's words played over in my head as we waited to see Vittoria Calogerà, my fiancée, make her appearance.

"You'll have to watch her like a hawk, Romeo, as she is cunning, my daughter."

A boast disguised as a warning. As the old man continued with an extensive list of her transgressions — interrupting himself now and then to remind me these were only the events he knew of—and finished up with the security measures he'd taken to control her, my disdain had more to do with his leniency than her willful behavior. No wonder the Calogerà family had fallen to such disgrace in so short a time. In my father's day, this man was feared, respected. Now, he was scarcely involved in his own operation, disappearing for months every year to private holidays in the old country. He'd become weak, a parody of his former self. The only real asset he had was his control over the east docks, and here he was, willing to give them to me — the son of his greatest enemy — if only I would marry his rebellious daughter.

"*She's been engaged before, you know. And her fiancée broke the engagement. I'd like to believe that she was being protected by her mother in heaven for a better man. But after three failed attempts to get her married and settled, I have to accept the fact that my beautiful, strong-willed daughter is a bit of a hoyden.*"

A bit? I'd had to bite my tongue to not laugh out loud. When I left the negotiations, I wondered who would get the better deal when I said yes. Sure, it may grant me the rights to all the shipping on the eastern seaboard and immeasurable wealth, but it came with some steep baggage, bogging me down with a mischievous, untamed bride.

Be that as it may, my cock strained in my pants when I climbed into the armored Audi A8 with Massimo following the end of the meeting. It was one thing for a Don to have a wife to breed with and run your household, but that wasn't why I agreed to take her off her father's hands. I wanted a woman of strength who was worthy of my name, and one whom only I commanded.

Vittoria was strong enough to keep me interested and also carry the weight of what came with our lifestyle. But in the end, I would break her down bit by bit, until she learned to follow my instructions to the letter. Obedience wasn't negotiable in our world, and it was time she learned that lesson.

Massimo had begged me to say no.

"*Are you sure you want to do this, boss? The Calogera family are no longer a threat to us. He's not trying to make peace here, he's looking for some sucker to take out his trash for him while it's still young and pretty. You don't need that headache.*"

I responded with silence and Massimo knew not to push me further on the topic. But even now, as I take him in my peripheral vision, I can tell he's not happy with this union.

I waited a full twenty-four hours before responding to Santo Calogerà, and his response wasn't disappointing.

"Romeo! I hope you are calling with good news."

He used my first name, like the deal was already done and we were already family, and he, the head of it. After I had shown him the courtesy of taking time to consider his offer, not taking her at the table like she was an object of no consequence, but not making him wait on coals for my answer either. At once, my tactics for playing out this conversation changed.

"That all depends, Don Calogerà. I am prepared for this marriage to go forward, but I have a few conditions."

He hesitated for the briefest of moments and when he spoke again, his tone gave away his desperation. "I'm afraid I have nothing else to offer you."

"So, you don't wish to hear what I have to say? In that case, I should hang up and we'll settle our peace another way," I warned, my voice steel.

"Wait! Please forgive me," he said quickly. "I am distracted this evening. Things with my daughter. You know how it is. Now you have my full attention. Please, Don Vitale, of course with such a solemn event as marriage, there will be additional terms. I understand completely. Let us discuss."

I smiled to hear the quiver of fear in his voice as he rushed to placate me. So he did know who he was dealing with after all, and he knew why they had nicknamed me the Devil. Now I had him by the balls.

"First, the wedding is tomorrow. No excuses!" I commanded over his stammering protests. "Second, she brings nothing from home with her. Not a damn thing except the clothes on her back. Is that clear?"

An audible swallow from his end. "You are not planning on mistreating my princess, are you, Vitale?"

I had to hand it to the old man, he had a drop of courage in him somewhere. Questioning me was like inviting the devil to send you on a one-way ticket to hell. Time to put him in his place.

"I'm not the one selling her to broker peace between us. You did that, so if anyone can be accused of mistreating her, it would be you. I'm willing to forgive that, but make no mistake, that is all I am willing to forgive. If Vittoria is to be my wife, I must do what you've proven yourself incapable of doing and bring her into line. You've allowed a pretty brat to embarrass and outmaneuver you, Don Calogerà, but I will not."

"But she is to have nothing? Rom — Don Vitale, I beg you for my daughter's sake, you cannot be so cruel!"

"You ought to know that I can indeed be cruel, but in this, I am merely being sensible," I replied indifferently. "When you get what you have always had, you behave as you have always done. By leaving behind all she has ever known, she will be forced to accept what I give her. Do you understand? She must be reliant on me as her husband and learn her place as my wife, and as she shows me her obedience, I will reward her with the privileges worthy of Donna Vitale. Now I am growing impatient."

"I agree to your terms, Don Vitale," he said in a frenzied rush, adding with a lame effort at humor, "but my daughter isn't used to being denied. She will be angrier than a hornet."

My cock swelled with anticipation.

"That is her problem. Not mine. Have her here at 7 am. The wedding will take place at noon."

I ended our call before I had to endure any more of his drivel. Then ordered Massimo to gather our head capos and make a wedding happen in less than twenty-four hours. There was a lot to be done in a short period and I wanted everything done precisely per my instructions.

"Don't worry, Romeo," Vinny had said during our tux fitting. "If she's a dog, you can always go bark up another tree."

My brothers had groaned, pelting him with cummerbunds and bow ties until voices in the hall turned us back into the grim, dangerous men we were expected to be.

Our staff, with my mother's direction, had done an exceptional job of making the cathedral-styled entertainment space resemble a lavish wedding destination paradise. But, when she began to work herself up over the timetable and the guest list, Vinny smoothly stepped in and took over the arrangements.

Vinny was my only blood brother not directly involved in the family business. He was a chef and owned his own chain of restaurants. But he didn't resemble a made man, or even a chef. Somehow, he'd inherited some recessive genes and instead of the dark brown almost black hair that the rest of us had, his was a dark amber blond that he kept longer than the rest of us. His curly locks were long enough to brush his shoulders and were often in some kind of man bun thing with the underneath shaved. More of a surfer from Cali than a mafia prince. When he showed a passion for cooking, my mother had begged me to allow Vinny to follow his passion for food. I'd never regretted it. His restaurants had hosted a lot of dinners long after closing hours, and washed a lot of dirty money squeaky clean, but at a time like this, I was grateful for his particular expertise. Where else could I get a wedding this size catered on a moment's notice? Vinny might not have a head for the family business, but he was his own kind of genius.

Now, as I waited at the altar, I glanced down the row of my best men, from Massimo ever at my side, Fausto the next in line, who ran our shipping empire, Giovani, who operated our clubs, Antonio, our numbers expert and head of gambling, Gaetano, a brilliant surgeon who ran a hospital and took care of our troops, and the baby of the family, Vinny at the far end. I saw my brothers, *mi familia*, my band, my blood. But I also knew none of the guests gathered today would see who we were, only what we were: seven hardened men.

The string quartet began the wedding march. A collective hush fell over the crowd, and then she stepped into view. It wasn't her succulent body that her wedding dress hugged in all the right places or her stunningly beautiful face, but the intensity of the glare she speared me with.

"You'll have to be careful with that one, brother," Massimo

whispered. "She looks like the type of woman who would carve out your heart and make you eat it."

Fausto, and Gio heard the whispered comment and laughed, then coughed to cover it up.

"Who knows, maybe you'll get a taste first, and what a taste! I mean, look at her! A veritable goddess." Gio whispered back.

At that moment, I decided two things. One: I would fuck the anger out of her until she was a pliant, biddable wife. Two: I didn't like anyone else looking at her.

Now I had new reason to be glad I'd made the plan I did. Because until Vittoria learned her place as my wife, she would be a prisoner. Lewd images of her tied to my bed as I sunk my cock into her and screwed her senseless captivated me as I watched her walk up the aisle on her father's arm.

I smirked at her, communicating my dominion over her as she passed from his authority into mine, and saw the heat flare in her eyes. I couldn't wait for the exchange of our nuptials to end, so I could end this sham and move on to what was real, her warm, soft body beneath my hardened one while I took her for the first time.

When she moved beside me, she was fidgeting. I grasped her by the hand and held on tightly, and wouldn't relinquish my grip until she settled.

"Too tight," she finally whispered for only my ears to hear.

"Behave, and I'll lighten my grip."

She rolled her eyes, but relaxed.

"That's my good girl." I crooned, more to piss her off than anything else.

"I'll never be yours," she spat.

"Oh sweetheart, you keep telling yourself that."

The priest began and as her father promised, she did her duty with none the wiser as to her true feelings. But I knew and couldn't wait to prove to her that even the brattiest little girls could be tamed, and this Daddy knew exactly how to do it.

CHAPTER TWO

Vittoria

"Papa, please." I begged, "don't make me!"

My father stood in the doorway of my bedroom while my maid hustled around the room opening blinds and pulling out suitcases. Apparently, I was to get married today, to a man I'd never met.

Papa ignored me, but directed a few terse words to my maid. "No need to pack her items, as she won't be needing them where she is going. Her husband will provide for Vittoria now."

I tried one more time to change his mind. "But Papa, who will take care of you? You know you need me. Who else will make sure you take your medication on time?"

It was a stretch, but I played the only hand I had left and held my breath, waiting for his response.

When he turned around, his eyes were cold, furious. "My medication? You think I am an old man who needs nursing, eh?"

"No, Papa," I mumbled, bowing my head.

His gaze softened and he came to lay a hand on my arm, wrinkled, but scarred and still strong. "I will be fine, *Colombina.* And you will obey me in this and do your duty to this family. I have allowed you to cast your other suitors aside, but not this one. There will be no escaping your fate this time."

He turned and closed the door behind him. The breath I'd been holding came out in a strangled gasp. *Little dove,* he hadn't called me that in years and only used the term of endearment when trying to soften the blow of whatever news he was sharing with me. It also meant that this was serious, and if I didn't come up with a plan quickly, I'd be married in just a few hours. Never going to happen, I swore!

My maid stood with her head down, wringing her hands in front of her. Her body language expressed my sentiments that today felt more like a funeral than a celebration. With her busy organizing brought to an abrupt halt, she appeared at a loss for what to do. Poor Lise, she wasn't much older than I, and her time serving me had been a dramatic one, but never had she looked so upset.

"I'm so sorry, Miss Calogerà."

"Don't be sorry, just help me." I moved to my walk-in and rummaged around. "First, I need a disguise, Lise."

No response.

"Lise?" I poked my head out. "A little help here."

Unshed tears glistened in her eyes.

"I can't. Your husband-to-be sent a small army of men to ensure you are escorted from the premises, and the staff have been told by your father that anyone who helps you will be fired on the spot. I just can't I'm so sorry." Lise turned and fled the room, leaving me to pick my jaw up off the floor.

A small army? Who the hell was I marrying? For the first time, a thread of panic wound itself through the fury and outrage tying knots in my heart. I had no illusions. I knew from a very young age what it meant to be part of the Calogerà family, let alone the only child of an aging Don. No, not a 'child'. A daughter. Not a son, who could take on the responsibilities and authority of the family, but only a daughter.

It was no secret that my role in the family was to someday further my father's prospects through marriage. Many offers had been made, and three had even come to a formal engagement before I'd managed to run them off for good. In a higher-ranking mafia family, my behavior would never have been tolerated, but despite his reputation for cruelty, my father was never strict with me. Indeed, in the last ten years, he'd scarcely been home long enough to notice my indiscretions, let alone punish me for them. I'd always been able to navigate around his half-hearted efforts at control to live almost freely. If it hurt my reputation, so much the better! Fewer suitors to contend with. I was not completely blind to the harm I might have done to my father's reputation as well, but he ruled his small piece of the underworld well, and as long as he did that, my place seemed secure.

But in our world, things are never secure. Winds change. Alliances shift. Sons start wars that daughters must end with marriage vows. I knew this, even if I never believed it would happen to me, but even in the highest families, surely the daughter would be told to whom she'd been sold! I had the right to know his name at least, and if I could get Papa to tell me that much, I could get him to listen to a few more thoughts besides. Perhaps there was still a way out of this.

I opened my bedroom door and made to step out when two large men in suits sporting holsters on their hips blocked me.

"Excuse me. I need to speak with my father."

"Sorry, Ms. Calogerà, but our orders don't allow for you to leave your room until it's time."

I would kill my fiancé with my bare hands when I saw him.

But right now, anger wouldn't help me get out of this room. I needed to think. "Was I also barred from having visitors?"

The men exchanged a look. Ha! I had them.

"Just as I thought. Please send for my maid to help with my hair." And before they could respond, slammed the door in their faces. I couldn't help the smirk. Finding a way to get one over on those apes in suits was inevitable. When Lise arrived, I'd soon convince her to help me, but as the minutes ticked by and no Lise was in sight, my smirk soon turned to a frown.

I worried my lip. Now what? *Think... think... you know what you have to do, Vittoria, just do it!* Nabbing my purse off the dresser I grabbed two credit cards and a bank card from my wallet. Pinning up my long wavy hair allowed me to hide the cards in the bird's nest on the top of my head.

I giggled, admiring the mess in the mirror. Let my fiancé behold his vision of loveliness. *Oh, good idea, V.* I patted myself on the shoulder. Digging through my closet at the very back under the last shoe rack was a pair of unflattering grey sweatpants and a faded ACDC t-shirt. I added mismatched socks and a pair of sneakers that had somehow escaped the garbage.

I wrapped a scarf around my hair and then tackled my make-up. Adding black and brown under my eyes not only made for some serious bags, but also made me look older and a little unhealthy. If all else failed, maybe my fiancé would call off the wedding himself once he got a good look at me. If he had so many men at his disposal, he must be rich, and rich men didn't like to settle for less than the very best.

Neither did I, but in my case, the very best meant being single, at least for now. No way would I obey some man just because he claimed he was the head of the household. Forget being a polite, obedient little wifey. Not this girl, uh-uh, no way!

I was running out of time, only fifteen minutes before the goons would collect me. With guards at every door, sneaking out the back of the house was out of the question. But, if I could get down the trellis outside my window in one piece, I could pass myself off as one of the gardeners working in the shrubs below.

I opened the window and peered down. It seemed a lot higher than I remembered, and the trellis was shorter. Previously, the lattice reached within a few feet of the ground, but my father had it cut halfway up in his attempts to stop me from sneaking out. As usual, he underestimated my determination, and I soon found other means of getting out unnoticed.

This right here, if I pulled it off, would be my greatest home escape in some time. Despite my excitement over a plan, my heart hammered as I slithered over the window frame and leaned on the edge until I could take my first step. I gripped the trellis when the worn wood groaned under my weight.

"If you live, Vittoria, no more pasta," I swore as I moved unsteadily down a structure meant to support flowering vines, not a human being. With each step, a creak, groan or crack made me hesitate. There was no point in attempting to escape only to fall and break a leg. I bet the beastly man would still make me walk down the aisle even with a cast on. But at this rate, my time would run out and they'd catch me before I made it to the bottom.

"Damn him!" I stressed my outburst with a stomp of my foot that went right through the wood. I scrabbled to find purchase with my feet, but the wood had taken enough punishment. Above me, the lattice pulled away from the exterior of the house.

"Argh!" My last cry lingered in the air as a strange calm settled over my panic. Closing my eyes to hide from the inevitable, my body floated, defying gravity for one moment. The air whooshed out of my lungs as I plummeted straight down.

At least if I died, there would be no wedding.

Whoomph! My breath slammed out of my body as I crashed

into the solid form of a person rippling with muscles. I cracked open an eye and looked up at the most handsome face I'd ever seen. His eyes were a smoky amber, like expensive cognac, and the expression in those smoky depths was primal and told me that he was used to getting what he wanted.

But as he spoke, his eyes sparkled becoming more gold and filled with humor. "That's a first," he said nonchalantly and gently placed me on my feet. "Do you make a habit of falling out of windows, Ms...?"

Oh, the man had a growly husk to his tone that had my insides flip-flopping.

"Uh."

His lips pulled into a smirk. "Your name is Ms. Uh?"

"How silly of me. It's Ms. Neapolitan." I grasped the first thing that came to mind, and it was ice cream. Not just any ice cream but my favorite flavor. Creamy and slathered with fudge sauce, smeared all over his —

I felt a blush snake up my neck and spread across my cheeks. If he noticed; he said nothing.

"Nice to meet you, Ms. Neapolitan. I'm Mikey. Well, Mike, but my friends call me Mikey."

Mikey was drop dead gorgeous. Now, why couldn't I be this guy's fiancée instead of... Hell, I didn't even know whom I was marrying.

"I guess you work here?"

"Hmm?" I startled out of my musings. "Yeah, I ah was leaning over dusting the mistress's room and leaned too far, I guess. Thanks for rescuing me."

"Is she ready, your mistress? It's time to leave."

Perfect! This guy was stupid. Super handsome, but what an asshat, falling for my lame story. I would have rolled my eyes if he hadn't been gazing so intently into them.

"Why, that is a good question," I purred. "Just let me hustle back upstairs and find out for you. I'll be right back."

I hurried to the front of the house. Standing there were my father and his guards, along with men I didn't recognize, who I assumed belonged to my husband to be.

Before I could bolt for cover, my father called everyone's attention straight to me, pointing at me like God in judgement as he bellowed, "There she is!"

Mikey gripped my arm and held me tight until the others came and hustled me into a waiting car. As the line of cars sped down the driveway, I peered out the back window and watched until Mikey and my childhood home disappeared from sight.

Great. From the frying pan and into the fire. What did that accomplish other than almost getting myself killed? I did meet Mr. Handsome and he'd proven to not be too bright. Maybe I could seduce him and get him to help me escape from the wedding. He'd be going there next, I bet. Sitting back in the car, I began to lay out plan B, escaping the wedding location.

Poor whomever he was would never know what hit him. It was hard not to chuckle aloud, but remaining quiet and angry was the best thing for now. Let them think I was stewing about being caught when really, I was tickled pink. By the time this day ended, I vowed I would be sipping a Mai Tai on a beach somewhere.

We pulled up to a set of gates set back off the road and surrounded by mature forest. Whomever this guy was, he liked his privacy. The gates opened and we pulled through. My breath caught when the home came into view. To say it was opulent wouldn't give it the justice it deserved.

I'd grown up wealthy and had anything I wanted, but this wealth was several steps higher than even I'd been exposed to, this right here was royalty. Suddenly, I had to know who had purchased me. Because in the mafia, marriage was business and often to the highest bidder. How my father had managed such an arrangement after doing my best to sabotage all efforts to marry me off was beyond me. Maybe he'd made up a lie like I could spin straw into gold, like in the fairy tale. Nothing else could explain the sheer opulence before me.

Appearing to be built in the late twentieth century, the home resembled an expansive villa, such as one would see touring estate mansions in Tuscany. But the Boboli-styled gardens were more reminiscent of Florence during the Renaissance. Whoever designed the gardens had created a marvel. The hedging weaved patterns to either side of the property with a huge fountain carved out in the center a few hundred feet from the grand entrance. Flowers and vines heavy with grapes grew abundantly in sun dappled clearings weaving an intricate pattern with it's surroundings. In short, the place was magnificent, and never had I seen anything like it... except I had. I'd seen this house, not one like it but this self-same house, on a recent episode of *Home Is Where the History Is*, a web-series that showcased heritage properties.

Try as I might, no amount of playback of the television episode featuring this home came back to me, except that I knew the owners name began with a V. Darn! Vigaro? No, Vitare, no, that wasn't it.

"Excuse me, but whose home is this?"

My handsome companion ignored me, but the answer swiftly became self-evident.

We pulled under the three-story high portico that extended out far enough to accommodate up to four cars in depth. The thick stone columns that held the enormous roof had a family crest engraved into their surface. I ran my hand over the image of the crest and the name Vitale. Hmm. It was Sicilian — Oh my god, not *the* Vitale, as in the greatest mafia don of all time, Luciano Vitale, and the sworn enemy of my family. *Oh, Papa, what have you done?*

It was too much for me to process. My legs went out from under me as I fainted away into waiting arms.

* * *

"Quick, bring her water," a beautiful voice demanded. I cracked open an eye to see I was laying on a massive bed in a room outfitted for royalty.

"Ah, you are awake. Drink this." The beautiful voice belonged to a slim woman probably in her early sixties, but didn't look a day older than fifty. Well cared for and groomed to the nines, she must be part of the Vitale family, as I couldn't imagine a servant so well turned out.

"Sit up, dear, let me help you."

I scooted back against a stack of pillows and allowed her to feed me sips of water from a crystal tumbler. The line of worry between her brows evaporated to be replaced with a resplendent smile, giving me a glimpse of the beauty she must have been when she was my age, a beauty that far outshone mine. Intimidated by her effortless elegance and assuming that was the standard in my new gilded cage, I squirmed under her scrutiny.

She noticed and leaned forward even closer to examine me, and was now near enough that I could smell her perfume, the pretty notes rivaling the beauty that wore it "Are you quite all right? You didn't injure yourself when you fainted?"

"I'm all right," I said automatically, then hesitated. Her concern and kindness seemed so genuine. Had I found a new friend and ally to help me escape? I took a chance and, despite the presence of several servants and guards sharing the room with us, I dropped my voice to a faint whisper, "No, I'm not all right. I was kidnapped."

"You don't say. How awful. By whom?" she answered with a slight quirk of her lips.

My heart sank, but my shoulders straightened and I immediately adopted my coldest and most authoritative tone: "I assume by a relation of yours. I demand to know where I am and be released at once!"

I suppose I didn't really expect her to leap to do my bidding as my servants would have done, but I also didn't expect this woman to chuckle at me as if I'd said something particularly witty over tea.

"You are delightful!" she said, rising from the bed to extend an inviting hand. "Welcome to the family, Vittoria. I am Isabella, and I am looking forward to getting to know you better. But that must wait until later. We have much to accomplish in a short amount of time, if we are to have you ready for my son."

Her son? So she wasn't just any member of the family, she was the widow of Luciano Vitale. That explained her reaction. She probably felt as threatened as a tiger by a kitten. I had no clout here and the sooner I changed my strategy the better if I wanted to escape.

I watched and evaluated everyone in the room during the fitting. I had expected they'd dress me like a meringue but instead, I was fitted into an Alessandra Rinaudo chic nostalgia lace gown with a plunging V down to my sternum. It was gorgeous and very similar to what I would have chosen for myself, had anyone asked me.

After the fitting, I was scrubbed, waxed and washed. Then more tea before hair and make-up. Of course, my contraband was discovered, but no one seemed upset or surprised. My father would have thrown a fit had he been the one to find it. Instead, these people smiled knowingly, like my attempts at escape were cute. Ugh! I may have met my match with the Vitale family.

I was still looking for an escape route when the first strings of the wedding march began. Crap! Now what? Nothing I could do but step through the opening and walk. I threw on my haughty face, the one sure to let him know I was not happy, nor would I be willing, and certainly not obedient.

In my peripheral vision, I noted the room and the gorgeous floral arrangements, but my eyes flew to the raised platform at the front of the stage, moving along the line of very handsome men until they landed on the groom.

No! It couldn't be! Standing with a smirk on his handsome features was Mikey, no longer laid-back and non-threatening, but one of the infamous band of brothers. He positively radiated power. I could all but see it pulsing in the air, mocking me and my tiny flicker of defiance. Well, I wouldn't give him the satisfaction of flinching. I lifted my chin, narrowing my eyes in challenge.

I saw one of the groomsmen speak and the eyes of my soon to be husband turned almost black. Even from this distance, I could feel his control reaching out and squeezing the nape of my neck. My knees knocked together and an unfamiliar feeling zipped to my core. Oh, I was in serious trouble with this guy and for an entirely unexpected reason: Somehow, I knew that if I stayed, I'd fall for him.

No! This princess would escape her new ivory tower and be free. I straightened my spine and started walking.

When I reached his side, he took my hand and gripped it tightly. Succumbing to his show of power, I finally let out a mumbling, "Too tight," wishing I could rub the spot I knew would bruise.

Smirking, he lessened the pressure. "Just a promise of things to come, my little brat."

"I'll never be yours," I spat defiantly.

"Oh sweetheart, you keep telling yourself that."

The priest began his litany, words that tumbled in and out of my ears without making any lasting impression until I heard, "— to witness the union of Romeo Vitale and Vittoria Calogerà."

"Romeo," I whispered mockingly out of the side of my mouth. "Mikey suits you better."

"A good all-American name for an all-American man?" he murmured back at me, his lips scarcely moving.

"The name of a common gutter thug," I shot back.

He chuckled, infuriatingly. "I'll remember that."

The priest droned on. Then came the vows. I responded when prompted, my mind and heart racing, like a firefly tapping frantically at the sides of an entrapping jar. Okay, so maybe I'd be married for a little bit, but then I would find a way to escape and get a divorce. In the meantime, sampling the goods wouldn't be so bad. He was gorgeous and just looking at the slight tick in his jaw told me he was as impatient for this to end as I was. Who knew, maybe once he got to know me, he would discover a shred of sympathy somewhere in his Devil's heart and let me go. A girl could dream.

But when the ceremony ended, instead of turning towards the well-wishers, he dragged me out a door behind the platform.

Servants scattered to get out of the way as he strode through the halls, dragging me with him, and at first, I was too shocked to resist. I'd never been manhandled by anyone and especially not one as gorgeous as my new husband.

New husband. The priest's words echoed in my mind: 'What God has put together, no man can pull asunder. I now pronounce you husband and wife.'

Fear skated down my spine in anticipation of what was to come and what this meant for me, and my self-control broke. I struggled as best I could, slapping and grabbing at doorways, but to no avail. His step never slowed until he brought into a room, not releasing his steely grip on me until he had closed and locked the door behind us.

"We have something to settle before we greet our guests." Romeo removed his jacket and placed it over a nearby chair. I had to bite back a moan when he rolled his sleeves and his fore-arms came into view. They were sexy, well-muscled and covered in ink. He curled his finger, bidding me to him and I did what any good, obedient bride would.

I grabbed the nearest heavy object at hand and hurled it at him.

CHAPTER THREE

Romeo

The Dom in me couldn't wait to taste her, while the Don demanded I instruct my wife on the subject of her new role. I knew she'd run the first chance she got, or at least try, and while I admired her tenacity, I couldn't allow anyone to witness me in a moment of indulgence. That would be for me alone to know until she could be trusted, then it would be ours to share, a secret that would ignite our lovemaking.

She fought me as I dragged her from the ceremony, unwittingly feeding right into my plan. Even on my wedding day, I could not afford to look anything but ruthless. My guests were, for the most part, my allies in the underworld, not my friends. Any perceived weakness in front of them undermined my power and invited a future attack. So I would let them think the worst of me. In my line of work, fear was the only thing keeping us at the top.

I kept my facial expression blank and hard, but allowed her to see the fire in my eyes. Vittoria was not a woman who could be easily cowed, and knowing she'd be a challenge made me hard as a rock. I hadn't met her before today, but claiming and taming the little brat was quickly becoming my obsession.

My cock pressed painfully against my pants. My entire body pulsed with desire and the need to own her in body as well as name. But all that would need to wait, for now, until after I punished her for this morning's childish misadventure.

I hadn't expected to run into her prior to the wedding, but a last-second impulse had me jump in the procession of security vehicles headed to her home a short time ago. Massimo, swearing, jumped in as well and attempted to lecture me on security details, at which I waved him off.

"It's my wedding day, brother. Let's have a little fun, no?"

He shook his head in disgust and turned his focus out the window. Poor Massimo, he was far too serious for his own good, and while I loved his dedication to keeping me safe, he really needed to lighten up a bit.

After everything her father had told me, flight was the most predictable reaction to her impending nuptials, so the first thing I had done after arriving at Don Calogerà's home was lock down potential escape routes. As soon as I saw what was left of the trellis on the west side of the house, I knew which window belonged to my young bride-to-be's bedroom.

I wondered how many times she'd used it before her father had finally noticed and trimmed it down. How many lovers had she secretly rendezvoused with? The thought angered me and I lingered there, eyeing the drop while torturing myself with scenarios. And then I saw her peek over the edge.

I ducked in close against the wall, under the frieze where she was unlikely to see me, even if she looked down, but she seemed more concerned with the possibility of people wandering in from the front of the house, where my car was waiting to take her away. I thought she might step out on the frieze and inch along it to another unlocked window, which would have been dangerous enough, but instead she climbed out over the sill and onto the trellis, clearly more willing to fall

*a good twenty feet from the bottom rung to the ground rather than
marry me.*

*I supposed I should feel offended, but I couldn't help the admiring
smile that spread over my face as I watched her make her way down.
Here was a woman of true courage and fierce spirit, willing to risk
everything for freedom. Dual feelings fought for supremacy as I contem-
plated what could happen if her recklessness led to a fall and respect for
her bravery, as misplaced as it was.*

*Clearly, Vittoria wasn't a woman who waited for things to work
out. She was a woman of action. Unfortunately, she acted before thinking, as evident by her current situation, which came to a rapid end when
the trellis broke beneath her.*

*I discovered I could also act without thinking as I darted out to
catch her, braced for the impact of a falling body, but when she landed
and fit snuggly into the cradle of my arms, all I could do was marvel at
the sheer perfection of how her body fit with mine.*

*Her look of shock allowed me a moment to decide how to handle her
and somehow, 'Mikey' came out to meet 'Ms. Neapolitan,' and it was
almost fun, the two of us, just talking. Maybe even flirting. For a split-
second, I was tempted to let her go, just for the fun of tracking her down
and keeping the charade in play, but my guests were on their way and
the Devil could not be seen being stood up at the altar.*

Now here we were, all alone for the first time. My eyes
scanned her from head to toe, her gown doing nothing to hide
the jewel beneath. The wedding dress showed off her perfect-
sized breasts and hard nipples. Her tight buds pressed against
the restraints of the silky cloth that barely covered them, beckoning me to pay them homage with my tongue.

It would take willpower to hold back, but right now wasn't
about taking her virginity, if indeed it was still intact. Such
traditional attitudes were still prevalent in my world, and
although I hadn't asked during our negotiations, her father had
made it known that he could not speak for her honor. I had
accepted this with a cool nod, tailored to intimidate, but in

reality, I didn't care. Honor was not lost in the bedroom, but built by actions, particularly as she did her duty as my wife in our social circles. Her wildness was not a moral testament, merely an opportunity to tame her to my liking. The past was the past and not worth worrying about, what mattered was that she was that now, she belonged to me.

Mine!

Her breath was coming in short pants, a blush on her chest and neck obvious against the white of her dress. My new bride might be angry, but she was also excited. I kept my eyes on her as I removed my tux jacket and lay it over a nearby chair.

Slowly, I rolled the sleeves of my shirt up. Her pupils dilated when she saw my forearms. She licked her lips as if turned on by the ink or the muscles, or maybe both. I curled my finger at her, almost laughing at the shift from horny haughtiness to prideful scorn in her expressive face.

Her eyes roamed around the room, darting from the doors to the windows, but I'd picked this room for a reason and the only way out was behind me. Then her restless gaze paused in a predictable place and I knew what was coming next.

She grabbed a vase from a table and chucked it at me. Her aim was good; my reflexes were better. I didn't flinch as it shattered against the wall behind me. She scrabbled to find something else to throw at me, but I was too fast, pinning both her arms behind her back, and pulling her hard against my chest.

"Tsk, tsk, little brat. Is that any way to treat your new husband?" I growled, and smiled as I felt her shudder and watched goosebumps break out on her bare skin. "You can fight me all you want, Vittoria, but in the end, I will win. Now, if I let you go, will you be a good girl?"

Another shudder. "Yes."

"Yes, what, wife?"

"Yes, husband?"

She was adorable, but when in private, I would be addressed

as Sir. The thought of her strapped to my bed or on her knees calling me Master was also rather pleasing. Daddy, Lord, King... Her knight in black armor. So many possibilities and all of them led to more depraved images. Christ, at this rate I'd be creaming in my pants.

"You will call me Sir when I desire it and right now, that is what I desire."

Her body relaxed and became pliant in my arms.

"Yes, Sir."

I released her wrists and slid my hands down her arms. "Good girl," I praised.

Stabbing pain in my shin almost brought me to my knees. Almost. The brat had kicked me with one of her stilettos. Play time was officially over.

"Thank you, wife," I said as I brought her kicking over to the bed.

"For what?" she yelled.

"For giving me the excuse to belt your ass. I was only going to give you a warning spanking, but now, well, I think painting your backside red is exactly what you need."

I pinned her face-down on the bed while yanking off her shoes. "You won't be needing these anymore. You have lost your shoe privileges for one week. If you fight me on this, you will also lose your clothing privileges," I warned.

She stopped struggling immediately.

"You wouldn't," she accused. The bedspread muted her voice, making her words come out sounding young and pouty — adorable!

"Oh, wouldn't I?" I put my mouth right up to her ear and growled, "Who did you marry?"

She trembled in my grip. "The Devil."

"And if you know that, I think you know there's nothing I wouldn't do."

I let her think about that for a moment, careful not to let

her know that she was right. Even the Devil had his limits, it seemed. I couldn't see myself forcing her to attend the reception naked. Barefoot, yes, but not naked. I told myself it was because I couldn't stomach the thought of another man seeing her that way, not to mention the consequences when some allied rival made a remark I'd have to answer with violence, but the truth was, the thought of her so humiliated only made me want to protect her from it. And in the end, even my reasoning didn't matter. What mattered was that she believed my threat.

"Our guests are expecting to greet and congratulate Mrs. Vitale. Being clothed for that is up to you, Vittoria. Obey me and do as I instruct, or I will take the choice from you. Understood?" I sounded harsh, like when I was speaking with one of my men, but she needed to obey me, and this was our starting place.

She stilled on the bed. I chose to take that as a sign that she would obey me, at least for the moment. I lifted my hand off her back and tugged her dress up over her hips. White lacey garters framed her gorgeous ass. The string from her thong tapered up to a V that kissed the dimples on the back of her hips. She was perfection.

I left the stockings but took off the scrap of material covering her opening and sat on the edge of the bed, arranging her over my lap, with her silk stockinged feet hovering in the air. I brought my hand down, a loud *crack!* rending the quiet of the room. I admired the handprint that bloomed on her pale skin, then made a matching one on the other cheek.

Vittoria gripped the bedding in her fists when the first smack landed, and after the second, she clung as if her life depended on it. I brought my hand down in a flurry of spanks, quickly painting her backside from pale pink to ripened berry. She howled and thrashed, but no amount of kicking and crying from her ended the punishment.

She didn't realize yet that she controlled the spanking. If

she let go and accepted her punishment, this would end, but letting go was difficult, especially for someone as strong willed as Vittoria.

I lifted her off my lap and onto the bed. Grabbing a stack of pillows, I shoved them under her hips until her feet dangled in the air.

"Don't move, Vittoria. This is your only warning."

I drew the belt slowly from the loops of my pants and folded it in half. The hissing of leather sliding over the wool of my pants as I pulled my belt free was the only sound in the room. In contrast, once it was free and folded in half, I snapped it. Vittoria twitched so violently, she slipped off the pillows.

"I told you not to move." I swung the belt, loving the loud sigh before it cracked on her quivering flesh.

"You bastard! That hurts!"

I almost chuckled when I heard the fire in her voice. My brat was a long way from behaving herself.

I swung the belt and struck the tender flesh at the base of her bottom.

"Ahh!"

Every stroke I delivered brought a litany of expressive words from my new wife, none of which were appropriate.

"Argh! You son of a —"

I brought the next stroke down lower, then painted the backs of her thighs a pretty shade of red to match her naughty little bottom.

"Ouch! I hate you!"

And on it went, with each stroke of the belt. Her ass and thighs were blazing red and would hurt for some time. But during her kicking and crying, her legs parted and I could see her puffy lips, slick and swollen with her arousal, quivering around the damp string of her thong.

I tore that last flimsy barrier away and struck those folds

with the belt. Vittoria squealed and gazed at me over her shoulder with a look of pure shock.

"I'm sorreeee," spilled from between her full lips. Her eyes pleaded as tears tracked her cheeks.

Not convinced, I struck again.

"Please, Sir, please, I'll be good, I promise."

I snapped the belt again, striking the soft flesh. A mix of a moan and cry broke from her.

"I don't want your empty promises to *be good,* Vittoria. I want you to promise to obey me, and only me. Do you understand now?"

She sniffled but didn't say the words I wanted to hear.

Time for a test. I took a few steps back from the bed.

"Come here, wife, on your knees."

Vittoria scrambled off the bed and fell to her knees at my feet.

"Take my cock out of my pants."

She reached out a shaking hand and unzipped my fly. She reached through the opening in my boxers and gripped my cock. Her eyes flew to my face in surprise.

"You're big." She pulled my cock out, the angry head eye level with her.

"Open your mouth and clasp your hands behind your back," I demanded.

She obeyed, and I quickly bound her hands with my belt.

I spread drops of pre-cum on her lips.

"Lick."

Her pink tongue darted out and swiped the cum from her lips, like a kitten licking from a bowl of cream. Damn, this woman was smoking hot and all mine. Just looking at her on the floor with her mouth open was almost enough to have me shooting my load all over her face.

I gripped her hair in one hand and fed her my cock with the other.

"Hollow your cheeks," I instructed, "and soften your throat."

I fed my cock into her mouth until the tip hit her throat. When she tightened with the pressure, I gave her hair a sharp tug. "Soften your throat, Vittoria, or I will spank that little kitty between your legs."

A guttural moan reverberated around my rod. She softened, and I shoved my cock down her throat. She convulsed around my rod and then relaxed.

"Good girl," I crooned. "That's it. Take your husband's cock in your throat. Feel me invading and taking what's mine, Vittoria. You belong to me."

Her moan reverberated around my cock, edging me toward my orgasm. A few strokes later, my balls tightened, and I pumped my seed down her throat. Gazing down at my new wife, I caught a glimpse of her beneath the surface for the first time that day.

With her white dress up over her hips, her heels resting on her naughty red backside, and her arms still bound behind her back, forcing her tits to jut forward, with nipples begging to be pinched — she was breathtaking. How I wished for the day to be over so I could feast on those gorgeous breasts.

Her pupils dilated as she gazed up at me, all the earlier hostility gone and only desire remaining.

"It's time to clean up and get back to the party, Vittoria. There will be plenty of time later to satiate that appetite of yours and christen our sheets with your virginity." I said, not knowing if she was a virgin or not.

Her cheeks went bright red with embarrassment.

"I'm proud of you, my *principessa*, for listening and obeying."

Her pupils dilated again. She liked praise and being good when acknowledged. Maybe the naughty girl act was just that, and all she needed was the right man to tame her. Only time would tell.

"Come." I held out my hand and helped her stand. "I will help clean you up, but then we must get back, so our guests don't wonder if you're still alive."

She paled with my words, but I meant it as a joke.

I grabbed a cloth from the bathroom and gently wiped away her smeared make-up. Without all the dark eyeliner from this morning and the excess from her bridal look, she appeared young, much younger than her twenty-five years.

I tugged out the hairpins and allowed her hair to cascade down her back in graceful waves to her hips. From the closet, I chose a simple black cocktail dress and beckoned for her to stand.

I pulled the wedding dress off and helped her into the other. "Okay, now we are ready."

"Shoes?" she asked hopefully.

"No. You were a bad little girl and when you misbehave, you will be punished. One week, no shoes. Understood?" I had stopped to cup her chin gently between my thumb and finger, capturing her gaze and forcing her to look at me. Her new husband and master, and the one she would learn to depend on for all things.

There was no animosity in her expression, just acceptance.

"Yes, Sir," she said huskily.

My cock hardened with her submission, and I hustled us out of the room before I changed my mind and ravished her right then.

CHAPTER FOUR

Vittoria

"These are my brothers, Fausto, Giovani, Gaetano, Antonio, and Massimo, and that one over there, is the baby of the family, Vincenzo." He pointed at a sexy young man who looked more ready to ride the waves than serve food. His ears must have been burning because he chose that moment to look up from the platter of something that smelled delicious in a large ornate chafer. My stomach grumbled loudly, and all the men broke out in laughter.

Embarrassment inflamed my cheeks and all I wanted to do was run and hide behind the closest floral arrangement. He finished ladling and passed the platter to a passing servant who was walking towards what I assumed was the kitchen. I liked to consider myself a very observant woman. You kind of have to be to survive in a world where nothing is expected of you but to shut up and look pretty.

I watched as the 'baby' sauntered over. He was more care-free than the others and less serious, yet there was a furrow to his brow like he was always trying to figure out a puzzle. He looked me up and down.

"No shoes? How very cavalier of you, Vittoria," he said with a smirk. I was surprised at his heavy Italian accent; it belied his looks so much that had I not known who he was, I would have assumed he was an actor playing an Italian.

Beside me, I felt Romeo stiffen. He clearly didn't like his brother's comment.

"Didn't you hear? Barefoot weddings are all the rage this season."

Vinny laughed and shook his head. "My brother is going to have his hands full. Welcome to the family, Vittoria." After kissing my hand, he sauntered over to a group of servers, stacking their trays with appetizers from the table, his demeanor becoming intense as he surveyed what finger foods they were taking out. We watched as he switched out their trays, speaking in rapid Italian. Once the trays were reloaded to his specifications, the group scrambled away to do his bidding.

"You'd never guess that hiding under that cool exterior was a perfectionist," Gio said, then winked at me.

"I take it you're not a perfectionist then?"

He shook his head. "Too much work. I like to live my life for me and not for anything else." He smirked. "Speaking of, there's Marko. I'll bring him over to meet you, Vittoria." He disappeared into the crowd and I saw him emerge by the entrance and embrace a tall dark handsome man. There was a message behind his cryptic statement and I hoped to find out what exactly it was.

To get out of this place, I would need help. With the right persuasion, maybe Gio would be willing to be on Team Vittoria.

"Who is Marko?" I asked no one in particular.

"His best friend," Antonio replied.

"Who invited Marko?" Romeo asked frowning at the two of them.

"They're inseparable, Rom, you know that," Massimo replied gently. "If you want him gone, I'll escort him out."

Before my husband could answer, I stepped in. "Let him stay. Look at how happy they are."

All eyes focused on the two men across the room, and I wondered if they were gay in secret. That was something that still didn't fly in our lifestyle, not even in 2023. While the world changed and grew around us, the mafia had their own set of rules to adhere to and while it wasn't spoken about, every boy and girl seemed to instinctually know that it was a big no-no.

"I will grant my wife's request. Let him stay, Massimo." His words were as smooth as honey, but the look he gave me was dark. And not for the first time, I wondered what monster lurked beneath that cold exterior.

Isabella came out of nowhere and joined our little group, laying a gentle hand on Massimo's arm. "Simo, can you get everyone's attention please?"

"Of course, Mama."

A loud whistle carried around the room, overpowering the guests, and the string quartet who had moved from the hall where our ceremony took place and set up closer to the banqueting tables to keep the guests entertained.

"*Attenzione*," he called out. Now I knew why she chose him. I don't think I'd ever heard a louder or more commanding voice.

"You have the floor, Mama."

She smiled and gently bowed her head gracefully at her sons. She was exquisite, their mother, and looked stunning in a fitted chiffon gown that brought out the amber-gold color of her irises.

"Lunch is ready. Please follow me."

Romeo gripped my elbow and led me into a massive dining hall, to a low dais at the head table, set for two. The décor matched that of the ceremony room, and the fragrant flowers filled the dining hall with the most pleasant smells.

Gorgeous hibiscus, white Anthurium, and bundles of tulips surrounded the head table. Calla lilies, delicate orchids, and vibrant peonies decorated the table. The arrangements were simply gorgeous.

Romeo pulled out my chair and tucked me in, but I wasn't fooled by his feigned gallantry. He may act a gentleman, but there was nothing gentle about him, and it was important that I never forget that, regardless of how he affected me.

I had caught a glance at the raw passion below his cool, calculating surface. Passion to fuck... passion to kill...

I suppose I had expected him to be more like my father, a Don with no time to waste on things, or people, that didn't provide him with power. My husband didn't hide who he was, but his true nature altered depending on the situation. So far, I'd witnessed the laid-back, laughing Mikey, the groom laughing with his brothers, the black-eyed Devil staring out at a room filled with dangerous men, the Master cracking his belt over my backside... and the man who called me his good girl and wiped my tears away. They were all the same man, and all true faces.

The entire day had felt surreal, from the moment my father entered my room this morning to my wedding in the most magical setting in the most beautiful home I'd ever been inside. It was too bad I couldn't enjoy it. I was a prisoner to a man I didn't know and, so far, couldn't manipulate. That was both terrifying and exciting for me; as a woman who prided herself in always being in control, the idea of someone else taking control held an element of desire. At my most base self, I wanted that big strong man that my mama used to tell me about when I was a little girl, as I pranced around our home in princess dresses dreaming of my prince charming.

But I locked that secret away and the only key was buried so deep, I doubted even I could find it if I wanted to. When my mama died, so did my dreams of prince charming. A year later, at the tender age of fifteen, my father began introducing me to potentially marriageable men in our circle.

I should have been a prize, a princess. At one time, the Calogerà family had been as strong as the Vitales, but the former Don had seized much of my father's territory, crippling his profits, and his increased absences over the last ten years had only whittled his standing away. Now he was seen as one of the weakest Dons and I, his wayward daughter. The true princes of our world had no interest in marrying into such a family. That left made men and petty criminals who didn't care about who I really was and only wanted keys to the empire. The very keys my father had presumably given to Romeo along with me.

To his credit, my father had to get rid of me somehow. After ten years of trying to marry me off, I had hoped he finally gave up, but as desperate as he must have been, I'm sure he never expected Romeo Vitale, the son of the man who had ruined father's standing, to come courting my hand. I had no idea what Romeo could have possibly gotten out of the deal. More power, presumably, although the Calogerà's empire was nothing compared to his. Still, it must have been something impressive to make him agree despite my bratty behavior... and if he thought he'd seen the end of that, he was sorely mistaken! I had no intention of changing who I was for him, but I'd let him think he cowed me, for now.

We took our seats to great applause around the room.

"Um, if this is where we are dining, isn't it a little far to get our food in the adjacent room?"

Romeo smirked. "Those are finger foods, Vittoria. Our cere-monial meal is being done in a traditional Italian feast."

Servers trickled into the room carrying platters of antipasto and placing them on the tables. When ours arrived, I took a moment to appreciate the artisanal display of the food laid out in the shape of the Vitale family crest.

"Wow, very impressive."

Romeo grunted but otherwise offered no comments, so I asked him a question, forcing him to converse with me.

"Why are we sitting alone? Is that a tradition or something in your family?"

Romeo's cool gaze held mine. "Not a tradition. More of a safeguard."

Huh? He thought I would run now, as in tonight? His thinking I could come up with a plan on unfamiliar territory that quickly, let alone that I was even capable of that after his punishment, both offended and impressed me in equal measure.

Our plates were removed and the next course arrived. I'd attended enough Italian weddings to know that I needed to pace myself. There were many courses in a traditional feast

Our personal server, a young man who looked a little like the Vitale brothers, brought out the *primo piatto*, or first plate—a pasta dish served between the antipasto and the main course—usually a Tortellini in a butter parmesan sauce, meant to help create a base for the lighter courses and large consumption of wine.

I took a bite and moaned out loud. In my peripheral, I saw my new husband watching me with interest. On my next bite, I held out my tongue and gently placed a tortellini on it. I exaggerated drawing it into my mouth and moaned while I chewed.

Beside me, Romeo adjusted his cock in his pants. Maybe I could seduce him after all. I continued to make love to the tortellini, while his plate remained full, so focused on me he evidently forgot to eat.

When the wait staff collected our plates, they found mine picked clean. My husband grabbed my hand and placed it on his hard length. He leaned towards me. But instead of speaking, he slid our hands to my crotch. Instinctively, I opened my legs, happy and relieved the front of our table was covered by a tablecloth so no one could see what was happening.

I grabbed my wine glass and gulped down half the contents in one go.

"Thirsty, *Principessa*?" His soft breath raised the delicate hairs at the base of my neck and down my arms. "And here I was thinking you were already wet."

A tiny shudder moved through me. My sore ass and slick pussy had tortured me from the moment I sat down and now Romeo was reminding me of my state of neediness. Like I needed reminding!

He inched my dress up with his fingers. Every new inch of exposed skin increased my need. I wanted him to shove his fingers inside of me, but I wouldn't beg. Now I knew why he left out the panties when he dressed me: he'd planned this all along.

His fingertip slid through my soaking folds. I wanted to push his arm away, but then everyone would know what was happening. I also wanted to grab his hand and shove his finger deep inside of me. But I did neither. I stayed still and allowed him to torment me.

The next course, lobster tail with shrimp in a light white wine sauce, arrived. Lobster was my favorite seafood, but I didn't lift my fork to eat.

"What's the matter?" my husband purred. "You don't like lobster?"

I didn't answer and folded my arms across my chest. Romeo pulled his finger away and I released a deep breath I hadn't known I was holding. He expertly cut my lobster and placed the perfect amount of shrimp and sauce on my fork, and cocked an eyebrow at me expectantly.

I obediently opened my mouth, and he slid the fork inside, waiting for me to close my lips before extracting the fork. It was so sexy, and I couldn't help the little moan that escaped with the succulent meat on my tongue.

Romeo took a bite and then fed me. He continued this pattern until both our plates were empty and removed from the table. Then he slid his finger back to my opening, pressing past my swollen lips and against the hardened nub hiding behind the folds.

"You were a good girl, Vittoria, and now I will reward you."

Expertly, he circled my clit as he took a sip of wine. I swallowed the gasp I so desperately wanted to release. This was so naughty, and the very idea was driving me toward an orgasm. He pinched my clitoris between his fingers. I grabbed my drink downing the second half of the wine just so I could moan into my glass.

Beside me, I caught a smirk on his face. Ugh! He loved controlling this, controlling me especially. He pinched again and a zap of heat traveled down my spine to my clit at lightning speed. I could feel myself about to let go, to give in to the pleasure, when he pulled his finger out with the arrival of a lamb dish.

Seriously! He just denied me an orgasm.

He cut a piece of lamb for me, but I kept my lips firmly closed. I'd show him how pissed off I was.

"I promise you it is worth the wait, but if you continue to be a naughty girl, there will be no orgasms. Now open for Daddy."

Daddy? I'd play along. I opened my mouth and when he slid the fork in, I clamped down before using my lips to pull the meat away. "That's what will happen to your precious package, *Daddy*, if you continue to provoke me."

I must have gone too far. His gentle tone was gone, along with his sexy smirk. Mr. Cold returned and was freezing me in place with his glare. I noticed that when his eyes glittered with danger, they also went a shade darker. All the gold flecks vanished, and the soft amber turned deep brown.

I glanced around the room, but no one seemed to notice that my new husband's demeanor had become glacier.

"Is that right, Vittoria? Could you bite my dick off without a second thought?" He leaned in so close his breath on my neck felt like fire. "You know what I think. I think you're a naughty girl who wants to be dominated. Every act of defiance today tells me you want my handprints on your ass and my cock buried deep inside you."

He leaned just ever so much closer. His tongue flicked out and licked the shell of my ear. "You want someone who will beat your ass and fuck you hard in the bedroom, then treat you like the queen. You can run as many times as you wish, but I will always find you, will always bring you back, and most definitely will mark you as mine every single time you get out of line."

My heart thundered in my chest and when he shifted back in his seat, turning his attention to his food, I felt the loss of his overpowering presence. I shivered although I wasn't cold. *I will always find you.* The promise in his words reverberated through me, sending all kinds of signals to my clit. I was royally screwed because there was definitely an attraction, a darkness in him that called to me.

By the time the cake was done, so was I, and couldn't wait to have a shower and go to bed. Romeo, either sensing or wanting the same thing, rose from his chair and took my hand. I followed him as we went to every table to say good night to our guests. The men jibed him about being in a hurry to deflower his new bride while the women offered me looks of sympathy.

An hour later, we were finally alone in his master suite. There was no evidence of the vase I'd thrown at him earlier. The room looked as pristine as when we entered it the first time. However, a thoughtful employee, or perhaps his mother, had turned down the bed. The blankets were folded, exposing a portion of white sheet decorated with rose petals as the Vitale

crest. These people really liked to drill it home. Yes, I got it I
was now a Vitale. *Mrs. Vitale*. Oh, the title sounded so foreign,
yet hummed through me with an excited buzz. Oh, hell yes, I
was Mrs. Vitale, married to the hottest man I'd ever lain
eyes on.

It was a nice gesture, but wasted on this loveless union. I
pointed at the pretty mess. "Why go to all the trouble? It's not
as if we like each other?"

Leaning against the door, Romeo chuckled. I couldn't help
but notice his confidence, it poured out of every pore of his
body. And what a body. I had to admit a part of me had been
dying all day to see him naked.

"Come now, Vittoria, we are wed. Are you sure you don't
like your new husband?"

He strutted towards me like a cat, a large and dangerous
one. He was prowling and I was his prey. *Dear lord, help me. Close
my heart to this man and help me escape.*

CHAPTER FIVE

Romeo

My father taught me from a young age that we would all die one day, that we should not fear death but that we must not seek it either. It may have been the only time he ever lied to me. Since meeting my new wife a week ago, I'd died a thousand deaths inside of her and all I wanted was to die again. More than money. More than power.

More than sleep.

I had always been an early riser, but like so many things, that changed after marriage. For some reason, I just wasn't getting enough sleep at night any more, and instead of waking before dawn, I'd taken to drowsing in my bed until morning light or Massimo woke me. But on this day, I actually was awake already when Vittoria carefully moved my enclosing arm and slipped out of our bed.

I let her think her stealthy efforts had been successful and that I was still asleep. It wasn't as if there were anywhere she could run off to. As far as she knew, the only way out of our

suite was through the outer room door, where two guards —
one of mine and one of hers — stood watch. And although I
didn't open my eyes, from what I heard as she rustled about the
closet, she didn't even try her luck with them. Perhaps she just
wanted a private shower this morning. I did have a tendency to
spoil those for her.

Sure enough, she tiptoed across the floor and soon I heard
the bathroom door softly shut. At once, I rolled over across the
spacious bed, stretching like a cat. I had work to do and no
doubt Massimo was already waiting in the office. I could easily
imagine him glowering at my empty chair, counting down the
seconds until I was late enough to warrant him interrupting me
with a text.

Maybe I ought to get up and show him I still knew where
my priorities lay.

But I had time to join my wife for a quick shower.

Grinning, I flung back the blankets, my cock already hard-
ening in anticipation as I gathered some clothes and headed for
the bathroom.

I hadn't heard the water running, and on some level, I must
have known what that meant, because I was distinctly unsur-
prised to open the door and catch my wife attempting to
squeeze herself out the narrow bathroom window.

I caught only a glimpse of her wide eyes and then her hands
must have slipped, because the next thing I knew, she was
wedged in the narrow window by her ample backside.

The picture she made, framed by the window and hung on
the bathroom wall, was almost as tantalizing as it was exasper-
ating. Almost.

"Naughty girl," I tsked, setting my clothes down and
strolling over to join her. "Escaping so soon?"

Her jean-clad bottom bucked as her legs kicked in a last
desperate bid to wriggle through, but it was no good. She tried
to wriggle back in next, but that was just as fruitless and at last,

she slumped over the skill, bowed but not defeated, her toes dangling several inches above the floor.

"Well, no, actually," she said sourly and looked back at me over the curve of her upturned ass. "I can honestly say that I am not escaping. Now are you just going to stand there or are you going to help me back inside?"

I thought about it.

"Romeo!" she snapped and slapped the wall.

"I love it when you shout my name," I told her and hauled her back in, helping her shift around to squeeze through, and set her firmly back on her feet. "Now what is this behavior? Have I not given you enough orgasms? How have I mistreated you? Come on, tell me why you think running away is justified."

Vittoria folded her arms defiantly, but I didn't miss the sudden blush on her cheeks, or the way the pulse at her throat throbbed. Heat furled through me. She smelled of roses and vanilla, and something spicy I couldn't identify, and all I wanted to do was bury myself in that scent and ravish her until she cried my name again, but I had to be stern

"Vittoria," I warned, unsmiling. "It is never a good idea to ignore me when I ask a question."

A flicker of guilt touched her eyes before she tossed her hair and served me a haughty stare. "I just wanted to go outside."

"Through the window?"

"What choice did I have? You've kept me in your room for a week now. When do I get to see other people?"

We both knew this was not what she was doing, but I would play along for now.

"All you had to do was ask. I will let your guards know that you wish to walk the property and they will escort you."

"Escort me?" she echoed indignantly.

I pretended to be concerned. "My *principessa* is not satisfied with the company of guards? Very well. Tonight, I want you dressed and ready for dinner with my family by 7 pm."

"Fine," she huffed.

"So that's settled," I said and placed my foot on the edge of the soaker tub, swiftly hauling her over my thigh.

"Romeo!" she cried out, flailing wildly for a moment before grabbing my shin.

As if I'd let her fall.

I brought my hand down on the meatiest part of backside, loving the loud echo that ricocheted off the walls of the bathroom.

"Ow! What was that for?"

I leaned over to stare at her until she blushed and rolled her eyes beneath the curly curtain of her hair.

"All right, so that was a stupid question," she muttered.

I tugged her jeans down roughly, her panties with them, and spanked her until her pale globes turned ruby red. During her endless kicking, they slipped down her legs and off her feet to pool on the floor.

I had a perfect view of her entrance, her hard nub playing peek-a-boo between her slick puffy lips. I slid a finger through her wet folds.

Vittoria moaned and parted her legs, looking for more.

I shifted my stance until we faced the ornate Italian mirror above the dual vanity.

"Open your eyes," I demanded. "Do you see how hot you are when you want my cock?"

I slid my finger inside her pussy. Her walls squeezed my invading digit.

"Look how your pupils dilate."

Vittoria watched her changing expressions as I finger fucked her slick channel.

I slid her off my thigh and pressed her against the counter. Lifting her leg, I placed her thigh on the counter and tugged her hips back. I pulled her shirt and bra off, and her luscious breasts hung like ripened fruit, begging to be plucked.

I grasped one and pinched her nipple as my other hand slammed against her ass.

She yelped with surprise, then growled as I smacked her mound. I rolled her nipple between my finger and thumb and alternated with my other hand spanking her ass and her pussy lips., bringing her closer and closer to the edge while expertly keeping her from the release she craved.

"Please, Romeo! Please. I need to!"

"You need to what?" I prompted.

She hesitated, closing her eyes as if by uttering the very thing she needed, it hurt her to confess it, but when I also paused, she was quick enough to stammer, "I need to cum."

"That doesn't sound like my *principessa* is asking," I remarked, smacking her clit so that she gasped and bucked in my arms. "That sounds like a brat who is demanding. Who do you belong to, Vittoria?"

Her heavy lids opened as she eyed me in the mirror.

"Let me remind you." I pinched her clit. "This is mine."

Pushing in my two long fingers until I felt the A-spot behind her cervix. I gave her a powerful thrust. "This is mine."

I pulled out of her and slapped her mound, hard. "This is also mine."

I spanked her ass with a flurry of intense spanks while she hung onto the ledge with a death grip.

"This is mine and I will prove how much right now." I opened the drawer and pulled out a container of lube. In the mirror, Vittoria watched me with a sort of morbid fascination, her lips slightly parted and her eyes opened wide, smoky with desire and bright with apprehension.

I squeezed a generous amount into my hand and lubed up her puckered hole. Sinking my finger inside her hot little backside, I pressed and massaged the tight ring of muscle.

"Oh!" she gasped and gripped the countertop harder.

I worked her back hole for a while, until she began to move

with me. My hand slick with more lube, I stroked my cock while I played with her, adding another finger, testing her limits. In the mirror, she watched, licking and chewing her bottom lip. So sexy.

Moving back behind her, I slid my cockhead into her anus, loving the look of pure shock on her face. Before she could protest, I sunk my cock all the way in. Vittoria froze with the intrusion; her skin glittered with perspiration.

I reached for her breasts and thrummed her nipples until she thawed. Unfrozen, she arched her back in invitation and ground her very warm ass against my groin, a sign that she was ready to proceed.

"Play with those nipples, *Principessa*," I ordered.

She slid her hands to her breasts, tweaking and tugging on her pebbled nipples.

Kneading at her ass, I pumped my hips.

"You're so fucking tight. *Perfezione!*"

I slipped my other hand down to her swollen lips and finger fucked her.

"Ahh! Oh my god! Oh my god, *Romeo!*" she shouted, slamming her hands down on the counter as her entire body shook with her orgasm.

I pinched her clit and watched in the mirror as a second wave tore through her. Her body quaked and clenched around my cock as she threw her head back, her mouth releasing a primal cry. Fucking gorgeous!

I growled with my own release, pumping my seed deep into her ass. When I was done, Vittoria collapsed forward. Holding her upright with one hand. I stepped into the shower.

Cradling her to my chest as the warm water poured over us. Vittoria seemed content to rest against my chest, completely spent, but I wasn't quite done with her yet.

"Who do you belong to, Vittoria?"

Her eyes fluttered open and gazed up at me. She was vulnerable, open, her heart as naked before me as her body, if only for a moment. "You, Daddy. I belong to you."

What else could I do but lift her into my arms and carry her back to bed?

And handcuff her to it.

"Have a good day, *mi amore*," I told her, stealing a kiss from her luscious, cursing lips. "I'll see you after work."

I had several work-spaces around the city, but the one I thought of as 'my office' was right here at home As expected, Massimo was there already and impatient to begin the day's business.

Gone were the days of dim, smoke-filled rooms with old men in dark suits at long tables, dividing the city like cake. My work could be surprisingly tedious between turf wars, with more and more of our family assets coming from legal enterprise, or successfully hiding behind one, most of it was paperwork. There were project reports to be heard, contracts to be approved or rejected, funds to be transferred and endless emails to be read. The hours ground out slowly and Vittoria was there, hanging over all of it like a ghost of perfume, beckoning me back to her.

"Rom? Did you hear me?"

My fantasies abruptly vanished with Massimo's question. *Of course not*, I wanted to rant. *Do I look like a man who gives a shit about anything right now other than being between my wife's legs?*

Aloud, I said, "Of course, I heard you. We have a meeting with the Bianchi brothers at three o'clock this afternoon."

"And this is you —" He gestured at me in my tailored dress shirt with the collar unbuttoned and sleeves rolled up. "— ready to go to that meeting?"

"You never heard of casual Fridays?"

Massimo scrubbed his hand through his hair before lacing me with a scrutinizing gaze. "You've been distracted to the point of obsession with this woman. Is she seriously that good in the sack?"

If only he knew. There was a time I would have told him, a time when Massimo and I shared everything. Simo was my best friend, and had been since my mother and I went to see his mother in the maternity ward.

I'd never forget that day, even though I was only two and half years old. I reached out my chubby hand to touch the sleeping baby. He opened his eyes and stared at me and I don't know, but it stayed with me because I had no brothers yet and felt weirdly connected. We stared at each other for a bit and then Simo had his first smile. Our moms filled the private hospital room with laughter watching the two of us watching each other.

From that moment on, it seemed we were never apart. He took his first steps holding on to my hands. My name was his first word. We grew up together and throughout our innocent boyhood, I led and he followed. Then his parents were killed in a territorial dispute, and when father brought him and his two brothers to live with us, our boyhood ended and we had to grow up even faster. We learned how to fight, how to shoot... how to kill. And girls, yes, we learned about them, too, and whatever we hadn't learned yet, we talked about even more. And through it all, Massimo was forever at my side, forever following where I led and eventually became my *consigliere*, who managed all the Capos of our extended family and reported to me directly.

Like us Vitale sons, the Di Mauras had no choice but to be part of this life, part of us. It was like fate had decided we seven would be brothers, and together we could weather any storm, even those created by rivals who wanted what we had, and there was plenty of those. But with my alliance with the Calogerà family, I had secured every corner of my father's... *my* empire.

The climb had been steep, as had the cost to get there, and the view from the top showed me only new problems and new enemies. We had the Irish, Russians, and the Yakuza, who had posed no problems to date, but I didn't expect that to last forever. Now that I was top dog, everything would change, even loyalties.

We dealt in prostitution, but not trafficking, that was the Russians. They had trains running all the time for their clients around the world. And their other great claim to fame was smuggling and dealing in arms, something my family had not been a part of, nor would they ever. The Russians never moved beyond their baser mobster instincts, and that worked out well for us. We'd grown, in both legal and illegal businesses and controlled the ports and now, all the shipping routes. We didn't have to deal shit on the streets to build an empire, because we decided what came in and out of the country. That was the true power and now it was ours. Sure, there would always be ambitious punks who thought they'd found the limits of our control, and that was the purpose of the meeting this afternoon; the Bianchis might think they were there to offer our man on the east docks their discounted goods, but when Simo and I walked in, they'd know their encroachments into our territory had not gone unnoticed after all, and we would learn who they were working for now.

"You're doing it again," Massimo said, interrupting my thoughts. "What is it this time? Her tits or her ass?"

"That's my wife you're talking about. And for your information, I was thinking about the Bianchis."

"Good," Massimo grunted. "Nice to know you can still put your head in the game when you have to."

But now that he'd brought her up, my thoughts strayed to Vittoria, to her firm full breasts bouncing as I fucked her, her luscious ass quivering and turning red as I spanked her. I couldn't help wondering if she was still as I'd left her, bound spread-eagle across the bed, or if she'd somehow managed to escape the cuffs. I knew she couldn't be loose on the grounds or the in-house security monitor would have alerted me, but if anyone could do it, my bride would find a way. I had to hand it her; the woman was tenacious. I was beginning to understand why her father had been so indulgent with her, even at the risk to his own reputation. However, there was real danger in her wandering off and I took this seriously and would correct her with very real and immediate consequences.

By now, everyone knew what the Vitale queen looked like, and if she ever managed to escape the home where I kept her protected, it would be nothing for my enemies to snatch her up. If that happened, everything I'd built from the legacy I'd inherited would fall, tumbling from my hands like a deck of cards.

The intensity of this conviction surprised even me. I'd never thought about the reality of having a wife until it became necessary as part of my transaction with her father, but now I couldn't imagine a life without Vittoria in it. Somehow, in such a short time, the Romeo I had always been — the son, the brother, the boss — had expanded to become the husband as well, and not only could I never go back to the simpler man I'd been before, I didn't even want to.

"You ever think about getting married, Simo?" I asked, musing on these thoughts.

"Why?" he countered. "We in trouble with another family already?"

"I'm serious. You should get married," I decided, pointing at him. "Loosen you up. If she's a sweet, obedient lady, you'll finally relax and have some fun. And if she's a hoyden like mine, you'll have even more fun."

"I don't have time," he said flatly. "And neither do you. We're meeting the Bianchis in an hour. Go put on a tie, kiss your distraction goodbye and meet me in the car. You make me come up and get you and you're riding in the trunk."

"Yes, boss," I said.

Massimo, already on his way out the door, stiffened and sent me a black stare for that, but left without further comment.

I left my office and made my way through the house to our suite. I'd left instructions with the staff that when the door to my private quarters was closed, no one was to go in. Despite that, an uneasiness filled me about that door. Would it be closed as it was left, or... Relief washed over me when I discovered the door was still closed and a guard still posted outside.

"Carlo," I said, walking up to him. "You're one of my wife's personal guards?"

"Yes, sir. Team leader, sir."

I was surprised that Massimo would give this assignment to Carlo, one because he was still fairly young despite having been with us since his high school days, but also pleased because he was a tried and proven soldier and had kept me from getting shot on more than one occasion.

"Good. I think it's time my wife met her security staff. Call your team, get them up here, and introduce yourselves. Then show her around."

"Yes, sir. Where?"

"Anywhere she wants. What's mine is hers. Just don't let her get too comfortable anywhere, keep her moving. You'll get a formal debriefing later."

"Yes, sir."

"Good man. Oh, and Carlo?" I reached for the door, but paused to lock eyes with him. "This is one of those jobs you really, *really* don't want to fuck up. Understand?"

"Yes, sir."

I entered our bedroom warily, prepared for anything, only to find my wife sleeping in her restraints. Quietly, undoing the cuff, I gently moved her arm, and ran my hands down her smooth skin. She moaned, her eyes fluttering open.

"Have you been here this entire time?" she asked sleepily. "I thought you had a meeting?"

"I do. I can't stay long."

Real disappointment flashed across her face, swiftly replaced by a haughty pout. "No one asked you to stay."

"Perhaps not, but someone is asking me for a spanking right now."

She stuck her tongue out and rolled protectively onto her back, the covers slipping down as she did so, revealing her beautiful breasts. I leaned over and took a nipple in my mouth.

"Mmm, that feels so good," she whispered, as she arched her back, and pressed her breasts against my mouth.

"Always trying to control the pleasure, aren't you, my little brat?" I said pulling back. "Unless you want a lesson in obedience, I suggest you be good and take what I give you. And since it seems your tongue is idle, I'll give it something to do."

A flush stole over her perfect skin, turning it a gentle shade of pink. I shifted her position to the edge of the bed, her head hanging, and her long hair dusting the floor.

"Open your mouth," I ordered.

Obediently, she opened her mouth. Unzipping my fly, I took my cock out of my pants and slid it into her waiting warmth.

"Mmm," she moaned against my cock, sending a wave of vibrations that made my balls tighten. I fucked her face and played with her pussy while she suckled me. When she came undone with an orgasm, it ricocheted around my cock. I came with a roar while she screamed with my cock stuffed in her mouth. Fucking filthy! And I loved it.

Pulling out and leaving a trail of cum on her face was the best ending.

"Time to get cleaned up, princess, you have a date with your new security detail."

Vittoria wiped her mouth with the back of her hand and rolled herself up to sit. "Really? Am I finally getting out of this room?"

I sat down beside her and pulled her onto my lap. "You are

mine. I've claimed every hole in your body, and you wear my ring on your finger. Do you know what that means?"

Her enthusiasm turned to suspicion in a split-second. "What?"

"It means, little girl, that if you don't follow and abide by all the rules, I will punish your naughty backside thoroughly and take away privileges. Losing the right to shoes is not a big deal when you aren't leaving to go anywhere. But imagine fine dining with no shoes? Or shopping?"

"You can't!" she gasped. "Besides, the stores and restaurants wouldn't allow me to go barefoot."

I couldn't help it. A great guffawing laughter erupted from me.

"Did you want to test out your theory? Please do. I can't wait to prove you wrong. And you haven't had a proper tour of my estate. You can't imagine how many heavily guarded spaces I have that could keep a little brat contained, and all a lot less comfortable than this plush apartment. Keep that in mind and let that help you make better decisions. Are we clear?"

"I guess so."

I wanted to bite that pouty lip of hers but there was plenty of time later. Right now, I needed to get back to running an empire, and she needed to get ready.

I spread her legs and spanked her pussy.

"Ow!"

"*I guess so* isn't an appropriate response. Try again."

"Yes, Sir."

"Good girl. Now off you go." I put her on her feet in front of me.

But she didn't scamper off as expected.

"What are you going to do?"

"I have a meeting and then I've got to go back to my office and finish doing everything I couldn't do earlier because I was spanking my wife."

She appeared unsettled, and not just at the mention of that morning's punishment.

"Is something wrong?"

She dropped her gaze to the floor, blushing. "I guess I was wondering if I could see where your office was. You know, so I could come to see you, or whatever."

"When I'm in my office, Vittoria, I am working. But that reminds me. I have a gift for you." I walked over to the walk-in and grabbed her new cell phone from a drawer. Handing it to her, I said. "I programmed this for you. My number, Massimo's, and your security detail's numbers are in there already. Carlo is the head of your personal team. If you need anything, you call him. If anything upsets you or you feel threatened in any way, you call me or Simo, understood?"

She nodded her head, her expression bordering on shyness. Combined with her flushed cheeks, she was adorable, a little girl trapped in a woman's body.

"What about a naughty text?" she asked. "Can I send that too?"

"You can text me anytime."

She lifted her head and smiled. "Okay. Thank you for this. Am I allowed to go on social media?"

I grew serious and pulled her between my legs. "Do you remember when you told me you'd seen my house on that show, but you did not know where it was?"

"Yes. I do."

"Well, there is a reason. No one can share this location with anyone ever, that includes whoever may pick up on your signals. Your phone is encrypted and secured, but is only for communication, not for playing on social media. If you prove to me you can be responsible with your online image, then I will get you a laptop. But you have to earn it, Vittoria, just like my trust. And when and if you do, there will no, and I mean *no* pictures of this home posted. You are married to the mafia king, and you need to conduct yourself accordingly. As my queen, I will expect you to be above social media, and as my wife, I will not share you with millions of others. You will grow into your role as you take up the responsibilities my mother is presently handling for you. If you need something to do, then check with her regarding a dinner party in a few weeks' time. She will walk you through what needs to be done."

She nodded, already a million miles away. What was she thinking? I'd give anything to have a window into her thoughts.

"Get dressed. Carlo will be waiting for you."

She scampered off, finally, and I left her to it. I couldn't wait to see how this day would play out. Either I'd be escorting her to dinner later, or tying her to the bed to be tortured with a vibrator at her entrance, teasing her for hours with no relief in sight. For a woman who loved sex as much as my new wife, that would be pure hell.

My phone hummed. Massimo, texting me a picture of the Audi's open trunk. My time for distraction was over. I grabbed a suit jacket and a tie and went back to work.

CHAPTER SIX

Vittoria

"No, no, darling. This way."

I nodded through a scowl of concentration, watching Isabella Vitale's slender hands at work. After my quick tour around the property — and by quick, I mean two hours because that is how long it took to walk the perimeter and detour through the elaborate gardens — I had found myself in the enormous kitchen, where Isabella invited me to share a cup of tea, and somehow her wistful reminiscing on her grandmother's pastries turned into the two of us attempting to recreate it. I had no doubt my mother-in-law would succeed. The only thing I was confident of making was a mess.

Although I hadn't been here long, I had already learned that despite her age and gender, Isabella was accorded a great deal of respect, not merely as the widow of the former Don or the mother of the present one, but a respect she had earned that was all her own. She remained not only an active force in the family dynamic, but in the running of her household as well.

She was a generous tyrant, gently correcting me with each failure, an iron fist in a velvet glove. I understood almost at once that while she lived in the estate, it would be impossible for me to take over as the reigning queen.

Now she leaned over my shoulder, tutting affably at my efforts. "So rough, *mia nuora*! When you knead the dough, it is like a lover's touch. Be firm, yet enticing."

I changed how I manipulated the dough. I imagined it was Romeo's cock I was massaging. Getting into the groove, I leaned further over the counter, extending my arms as I pressed the dough away, then with a firm grip, I drew it back to me.

"That's it," my mother-in-law encouraged me. "Feel how it responds to you? Feel it warm and become supple."

Immediately, my cheeks burned pink with embarrassment. I wasn't used to being watched by another woman, and certainly not the mother of my husband.

"Keep going, and just like when you're making love, you'll know the moment the dough is ready to be molded into something else, in this case, a shell to hold the juicy load of fruit."

Holy Crap! Was it her intention to have me thinking about sex? I felt a zing down to my clit with the naughty images assaulting me as I played with the dough. The song *After Dark* by Tito and Tarantula played in my head and encouraged my imagination to greater depravity.

I bit my lip to hold back a moan and excused myself to use the bathroom. A tinkling of Isabella's laughter followed me as I raced out of the kitchen for Romeo's office. He should be back from his meeting by now. I grabbed the phone from my pocket and checked the time. 5 pm and not a word from him. Panic slithered down my spine. Was he okay?

I walked quickly along the Italian marble flooring towards the front of the house where I'd been shown earlier his office was. By the time I found the door, I was desperate to feel him inside of me.

When had I become so controlled by base desires?

Really Vittoria? Isn't running away a base desire?

Shut up, stupid thoughts!

Never had I needed to feel the touch of any man. But Romeo infiltrated every pore of my being and moved in, filling every nook and cranny. I was valiantly working to keep him out of my heart, not wanting to love someone who couldn't love me back.

"It's just business, my father had said. *You'll find your way and carve out a life for yourself, Vittoria.*

But as I knocked on the door, an overwhelming need to know he was home safe and in one piece slammed into my heart.

I knocked tentatively.

With no response, I put my ear to the door and knocked harder. "Romeo! Please answer me!" My voice came out sounding more desperate than I liked, and perhaps it was that vulnerability that attracted the predator within, for my call was answered.

The door flew open and there stood a beast. It was still my husband, but an aspect of him that I hadn't seen before. There was no light in his eyes, only black pools where his humanity once shone.

"Vittoria," he growled.

I reached out a hand to cup his face, and he gripped my wrist before I touched him.

"If you stay, I will fuck you any way I please and it won't be gentle."

A shiver raced through me, settling between my thighs. A pool of moisture soaked my panties.

Like any predator, he picked up on my scent. A primal glint flared in the dark apertures of his eyes, and I knew there was no turning back.

I stayed still, the prey before the beast, waiting and willing to be slaughtered. But also, held my gaze steady. I may be terrified of going down this path, but he didn't need to know that.

"Words are cheap, Daddy," I said and tossed my hair. "Show this girl some action."

He gripped my hair and tugged me tight to his front. "Don't say I didn't warn you."

Pulling me into his office, he slammed my back against the closed door as he locked it. Gripping my blouse, he ripped it down the middle, the two halves fluttering for a moment before landing at his feet.

Holy shit!

My bra was his next victim, shredded into lacy strips he used to tie my hands in front of me. "I'm going to fuck you, Vittoria, until you're not even capable of standing." He tossed me over his shoulder, crossing the room in long strides, and cleared his desk in one sweep of his arm. scattering papers everywhere.

I shivered, ready to be laid out and ravished, but where it would have been easy for my husband to tip me forward and onto my back, he instead swung me around and dropped me belly-down over his desk, my bound wrists forcing my arms to extend in front of me, my hands grasping at the edge for dear life.

"What's this, wife?" His hand cracked against my jeans.

The thick muffled sound of skin on denim had enough sting and heat to send a message to my clit. 'You're soaking for me, right through your jeans." He shoved the garment down to my knees and my drenched panties went with them.

"So fucking wet," he growled.

Before I could comment, he shoved his cock inside of me, sinking to the hilt with one thrust.

A garbled squeak escaped me with the sudden, but not unwelcome invasion.

"You like being Daddy's dirty girl, don't you, wife?"

My moan was his only answer, but that wasn't good enough for him.

"Say it!" he commanded, seizing a fistful of my hair and yanking my head back so that my lustful cry filled the room. "Say it!"

"Y-Yes!" I stammered, my blush burning my face as a very different kind of heat pulsed in my core.

"Yes, what?" He pulled out and spanked my naked backside. I yelped aloud with the sting, but it quickly morphed into a fire that threatened to engulf me. "I can't hear you, brat. Answer me or I won't let you cum."

"Yes! I love being your... your dirty girl!"

"And you love my cock, don't you, my little slut?"

"Yes!"

"Yes, what?" he thundered, yanking on my hair until I could see him towering behind me, a Devil haloed by the office lights.

"Yes, I love your cock!" I shouted dizzily, "I'm Daddy's little slut and I love your cock! Please, Sir! Please let your dirty slut cum for Daddy!"

I cried out as a tidal wave crashed through me and I screamed as Romeo slammed back inside of me. The orgasm was so fast it took me by surprise and I wanted to ride the wave, feeling every ounce of pleasure, but Romeo's cock continued to piston inside of me. I was out of breath, unable to move. I could only lay limp and let him use me as he pleased.

He sunk a thumb into my ass, and I cried out as another torrent of pleasure ripped through me. His hand struck my ass, searing his print into my flesh. I cried out but he kept going.

Yes, my body screamed. *More! Take me hard and leave nothing behind.* As usual, Romeo heard my unspoken need. His hand slid under my chest and gripped my sensitive peak, twisting the nub between his powerful fingers.

"Oh! My! God! *Yes!*" My body erupted into a million pieces and as I shattered, Romeo roared with his release, filling my hot channel with his seed. I lay on the desk gasping, but he wasn't done.

"You'll lick my cock clean." He placed me on my knees and I instantly obeyed, opening my mouth. It was a blessing in a way, that he was taking the lead. My body was shaking with the intensity of our intercourse.

He placed his dripping cock head inside my mouth.

"Mmm," I moaned. He tasted both sweet and salty, the blend no doubt of our shared release.

He held the sides of my head, fucking my mouth with his semi hard cock. A few stokes later, his cock lengthened and he slid it past my defenses and down my throat.

I choked and he pulled back, gazing down at me from above with a smirk of satisfaction. I could only imagine what he must be seeing: Saliva and semen dripped down my sweaty, flushed face onto my bare breasts, my damp hair hanging over my lust-glazed eyes, mouth open and breath heaving.

"You look so fucking gorgeous wearing my cum on your face, *Principessa*."

His words were so dirty that despite being satiated, my clit throbbed for more. I moaned as he fucked my face, completely at his mercy and loving every second of it. If I'd known sex could be this good, I may have had it more than once or twice. What I'd experienced before was nothing like this.

His cock hardened and lengthened, gagging me as I worked to relax my throat. But just as I adjusted to the invasion, he pulled out.

Tugging me to my feet, Romeo lifted me onto the desk, placing me on all fours, spreading my thighs apart. Gripping my hips in his strong veiny hands, he thrust his raging hard-on between my quivering slick lips and sunk home. Once he had the rhythm he wanted, he reached under my body, grasping my breast, his finger squeezing the sensitive buds.

I shuddered as an orgasm ripped through me, soaking his

cock. He pulled out and pressed his cock head inside my rosette and past the tight ring of muscle, filling my ass. I fought the invasion until he spanked my clit.

"Oh!" The sting stole my resistance and he sunk all the way in.

"Hang onto the desk, Vittoria."

I did, gripping the edge tightly as he rode me. It was a savage invasion, just like he said it would be. What he didn't say, was how much I'd love it. The burn as he took what he wanted from me tipped me over the edge.

My muscles tightened as my pussy spasmed. Romeo grunted and then held my hips in a death grip as he unloaded for a second time. When he pulled out, his cum dripped onto the desk before I could close my legs.

He was right when he said he'd fuck me until I couldn't stand. I lay draped over his desk, not an ounce of energy left in my body. I heard him moving behind me then he gathered me in his arms, not saying a word.

Romeo pressed a panel hidden behind a book on his extensive book shelving and a secret door opened. I wanted to ask him why he had a secret door, and where it led but I had not the energy to say or do anything and allowed him to carry me.

I imagined I was Belle, and he was the Beast.

"That's my brother."

Huh? Did he just read my mind? Or had I spoken aloud without realizing? I was about to ask which brother had earned the title of the beast when he pressed on another panel. A door slid open and we were in our bedroom.

"What the hell?"

Romeo chuckled. "Watch your language, or you'll be over my lap getting your ass tanned."

"You can't tan my ass for saying hell," I said and crossed my arms.

He walked us into the bathroom. "I can do whatever I want,

Vittoria. You're mine. And I will punish you when you warrant it. You should have figured that out by now."

Hmph! Note to self... say whatever the hell I want when he wasn't around. I had to suppress a smirk. I loved defying those who thought they could control me. I hadn't given him a good dose of Bratty Vittoria because I'd been earning my way out of the bedroom and into the rest of the house. Now that I'd toured the grounds, counted the cameras and memorized the position of the household guards, I could make a plan.

"Yes, Sir." I saluted and accepted his triumphant smirk with a smile of my own. For now, it served me better to let him think I was his obedient girl all the time and not just when we fucked, but my end goals hadn't changed. Although there were aspects of my captivity that I enjoyed, and people I knew I'd miss, my best life was still waiting for me outside these windows and I still meant to find it.

I wondered how far he'd go to get me back. Would he do anything? Go anywhere? The intensity of his possessiveness would have been thrilling if it was really me he wanted so deeply. But to a Don like Romeo, I was simply a byline of a business transaction. He'd go after me the same way he'd reclaim an occupied port or stolen shipment, simply because he didn't like anyone else playing with his toys, touching his goods or defying him in any way. I could use that against him by taking a page out of Niccolò Machiavelli's book on warfare, or just reading *Cosmopolitan*. The magazine was as good as any tactical guide when it came to getting one over on a man.

CHAPTER SEVEN

Romeo

Exposing the secret passage from the office to our wing on the second floor had been a risk, but one I wanted to take. More than anything, I wanted to test out my bratty bride and discover her true motivations. I didn't believe for one moment that I'd cowed her into obedience, despite the spankings she earned each night.

Earned and enjoyed. Despite her verbal protests each session, her inner thighs shone with her desire. Slapping her slick entrance brought convulsions of excitement. Oh yes, she could protest all she wanted, but her body said something else entirely. Her need for the pleasure I delivered grew each day, and with it my ability to harness and control her.

When she banged on my office door, desperate for me to open it, I hesitated. Her *please* plucked at more than my desire to sink into her warmth. She called to me as a man, her man, and that was a first for me. Not just with her, but in all my life.

Being who I was, and what I was, sex without entanglements was the way to go. My previous relationships, if they could even be called that, amounted to having my needs of the moment serviced by some girl or another at the many clubs Gio managed for the family. It was better that way, safer. Even my father, a family man that loved his wife, had satiated himself many times prior to and during his marriage, lest his affection for my mother make her a target for our enemies. My mother was expected to understand, and even to socialize with his mistresses at gatherings. If it bothered her to share my father with other women, I never saw a sign of it.

This wasn't an unusual phenomenon in our world and happened more commonly than not. Yet I was not my father, and I did not subscribe to many of the old traditions of the mafia men who had gone before me. Despite not feeling more than a physical desire for Vittoria, I had no intention of living a double standard with her. I was determined to live the vows I had taken on our wedding day, until death do us part.

Opening the door, and trying to hold the beast at bay, at least until I knew she was okay, was also a first for me. Our life, this lifestyle came with a high cost, and being the Don meant I put the empire before individuals. So far, I'd been lucky, and while hard on my brothers — some, like Gio, more than others — I hadn't been dragged down that hole of having to choose our existence over any one of their lives.

And that was the crux of my issue with Vittoria. If I held her at bay, or rather, kept my heart wrapped up tight, maybe I could remain unscathed by shouldering the responsibility of having her in my life. We were compatible in many ways. She understood the necessity of preserving the family honor. Despite her wild history, when the time came, she had walked up that aisle to stand beside me, furious but obedient... in public, at least. I knew that if things got ugly, she wouldn't faint away, but fight at my side to defend the family in any way she could.

And in addition to the benefits of marrying a mob princess, there was our sex life. In the time since our wedding, she had volunteered the admission to having had two lovers before me, boys with whom sex had been boring and unremarkable, leaving her with no desire to experience it again. The confession pleased me, because I hadn't asked, willing to let the past be the past. She had freely given it because she wanted a clean slate, to belong to me and only me. I had cracked her open and shown her more pleasure in the few weeks we'd been together than she'd ever experienced before.

This made it very clear to me that the sex kept her in line more than anything, although losing privileges was a close second. My princess didn't like to be without her creature comforts.

"'Romeo! Please answer me!'" she'd cried, yet still I held onto a semblance of control, letting her know that to enter the lion's den meant she had no say in what went down.

My wife held me with a challenging gaze — "'Words are cheap, Daddy. Show this girl some action.'"

The last thread of restraint snapped with her sassy comment. Grabbing her, I slammed the door and pushed her into it.

Desperate to consume her, I shredded her shirt, and as the two pieces of silk white material floated to the floor, I was a visual of the darkness I was experiencing, a force consuming the light, in this case, drowning out and satiating my deviant bride until she couldn't stand.

Her sweet nectar was overpowering, pulling me in, demanding — *take me, I'm yours.* I bound her wrists with her lacey bra. I wanted to bite and mark her breasts, but my cock was so hard I had to release it from the confines of my pants.

Tossing her on my shoulder, Vittoria gasped, not with surprise. No, her sounds were a beacon, a calling — *show this girl some action.* Oh, would I! Clearing my desk with a vicious swipe, I placed her down — *Mine!*

Her hands bound in front of her, fingers clinging to the edge of the desk. She was ready. I smacked her ass, loving the sound of my hand connecting with her denim-clad ass. Sweet nectar assaulted my nostrils. I ripped her jeans down in one swoop, her panties with them. She was soaked!

With one mighty thrust, I sunk my cock deep inside of her. Vittoria's walls quivered with the invasion, her slick pussy doing its best to accommodate my size.

"You like being Daddy's dirty girl, don't you, wife?"

She loved it when I talked dirty to her, and she didn't disappoint; her walls spasmed around my cock. She was so close to a climax, but she wasn't allowed, not just yet. With reluctance, I pulled out and spanked her ass. She yelped but widened her legs in response. It would be so easy now to just tip her over the edge...

"I can't hear you, brat. Answer me or you will not be allowed to cum.

"Yes. I love being your dirty girl!" She gasped, arching her hips, and presenting her ass in my direction.

"And you love my cock, don't you, my little slut?"

"Yes!" she cried out.

I slammed between her wet swollen lips and she screamed, milking my cock with her muscles as a powerful orgasm overtook her. But this wasn't about her pleasure. No, this was about showing her what it meant to taunt the darker aspect of my personality.

Not breaking to give her time to recover, I sunk a thumb into her tight ass, and kept up my pace with my cock. She stopped thrusting, yearning and stayed still, letting me set my pace, and I did, my cock enjoying her soft tight channel and scraping the edges of her nerves with my size. She mewled, gasped, cried out and begged, for what, I doubt she knew. I slid a hand under her chest and pinched her nipple hard. Vittoria cried out. Her walls squeezing me so tight, set off my release. Howling I pumped inside of her. But I wasn't done...

Being distracted by her was becoming an issue. Not for me, but Massimo was not happy about the carnal bliss I was enjoying.

"She's distracting, Rom. Put a baby in her and let's get back to business," he'd said not an hour ago. Although babies were highly celebrated, it wasn't my purpose in claiming her as my bride.

She presented a challenge I wanted to control. And fucking her had become my new favorite hobby. I was seriously considering finding her for some afternoon delight when I spotted her walking past the window with one of her security. She pointed to something and her guard looked and laughed at something she said.

What the fuck?

White hot anger flared in my chest as I watched them until they disappeared out of sight. There was a closeness in their interaction that bothered me. I left the office through another panel and headed down a level. Here was where the real action happened. Everything above this floor was catered to family and pretense. Everything on this floor was the dark and dirty of my world. The security was high and so were my expectations.

I slammed open the door of the security room to find my tech guy busy eating lunch and texting on his phone.

"Out!" I yelled. I locked the door after him and watched her through the lens of every camera angle offered of the gardens. He was too close to her. Their arms bumped and yet she didn't pull away. Who was this asshole? He was new, but surely he'd been educated on the cost of touching the Don's wife?

I pulled my phone out of my pocket and called Massimo, who had handled the hiring of Vittoria's new security detail. A few of the men had been with us for years, and a few others, were taken from other positions in our massive organization and were not as well known to me. "Where are you?" I barked.

"Just pulling in. Where do you need me?"

"Security room, now!" I barked and hung up.

Soon, the door flew open, Massimo panting as he stepped through. "I'm here. What's going on?"

"That —" I pointed to the screen. "— is what the fuck is going on."

Massimo stared at the bank of screens, his gaze traveling from one to the other. "What am I missing? Nothing seems out of place."

I wanted to rip his fool head off and yell at the top of my lungs. But that wasn't who I was. I hadn't been reduced to losing my cool about a woman in front of others, yet.

"Who is he and why is he touching my wife?" I couldn't hide the possessiveness in my tone. *My wife!*

Massimo returned his attention to the screens, watching the pair. "That is Theo, her personal guard and if I had to guess, I'd say he's being friendly."

"Or flirting," I said darkly.

Massimo served me a look of annoyance almost bordered on a glare. "You think I'd put a man on your wife's security team if I wasn't dead sure he could stand naked in the shower with her and wash her tits without getting hard? My men do their job, Romeo, and so the fuck do I."

The jealous heart of me kept beating as hot as ever, but he was right and I knew it.

He spared me an apology, offering before I could speak, "Regardless, do you want me to move him elsewhere in the organization?"

"Put him on guard duty at the docks. If he complains about the demotion, then send him away, Antarctica, or six feet below, I don't care."

What the hell was going on with me? I leaned back in the

chair, one leg crossed over the other in the posture of a relaxed man, but my body betrayed my nerves; my foot tapped air and my fingers drummed on the desk. I despised those rare moments when I let my true feelings show, but Massimo knew me too well to have been fooled even if I'd been motionless.

Massimo's dark gaze turned inquisitive. "Rom, I haven't seen you this worked up since the news about your father. What's going on?"

I slammed my foot to the floor and pushed away from the desk. "Hell, if I know, Simo. I don't understand these emotions that are turning me into a paranoid pussy. Please tell me this is just lust and I'll be over it soon."

My brother's face split into an uncharacteristic grin. "Oh Rom, you got it bad. I'm so sorry, brother."

On full alert, I sat forward in my chair, almost upending it and landing on my ass on the floor. "What? What do I have?"

Simo laughed so hard, he filled the room with his rare display of laughter. If he were anyone else, I'd pull out my gun and shoot him, but his laughter was infectious and soon I was laughing right along with him, glad there were no witnesses.

"Brother," he said wiping the tears of merriment from his eyes, "I have to inform you that you are in love."

No! No way in hell was I in love with that little brat. She was entertainment, and that was all I needed her for. Simo was lying. He had to be... right?

"You know lying to your Don can get you killed. Don't make me kill you, brother, I would miss you."

Massimo calmed down, leaning back in his chair with his terrifying enforcer mask back in place.

"Come on, Romeo, are you telling me you can't conceive of being in love with your wife? I know you don't like distractions, but Vittoria is perfect for you in so many ways."

Ha! Now I had him.

"Really, how so?" My voice had taken on an edge, one that

was a warning not to push me and although it served me well outside of the family, Massimo generally ignored it. He was the only one I allowed to push me, just a bit, because he knew me better than anyone else. Had we been born twins instead of being brothers from other mothers, maybe we'd be running this empire as equals right now. As it was, I'm two years his senior and a Vitale, while he was a Di Mauro.

"She's a bit of a brat and likes to test you."

"*Pfft!* Does she ever, but I hardly see how that is a valid point."

Massimo continued as if he didn't hear me. "She isn't afraid of you, and that's a first for you. She challenges you and you like to be challenged, at least in the sack you do. Remember that one at the club who you liked playing with the most until she found the guy of her dreams and married him? She used to play the brat and test you. As I recall, you loved it."

Okay, he had a point there.

"And... she was raised as a princess, to one day be a queen. She has the right breeding and by the way you prowl after her, I can only imagine she's good in the sheets."

I processed his words and heard the grains of truth.

"I'll admit, she is all those things, but that doesn't mean I'm in love with her. Just that I hold her in high affection. And that is where I plan on keeping her, Simo, in a position of affection, and not one where she has wiggled into my heart. I'm not a nice man and don't plan on changing who I am or what I do. She can fall in line, do what she's told, end of story!"

Massimo regarded me but didn't speak.

"Now that's settled, let's discuss security. Soon, my wife will be given permission to leave the property for short outings when properly escorted, and that means no less than a security team of four, Massimo, I mean it!"

"I hear you," he said mildly, straightening up to a professional posture. "What do you need from me?"

"I'm seeing dead spots that the cameras aren't covering," I said, gesturing at the monitors. "I want those dealt with, and I need a stack of tracking chips. I don't completely trust that my wife will stay with her security team. The better tracked and protected she is, the more I can turn my attention elsewhere."

If Massimo had seen through my act to what lay beneath regarding my feelings for Vittoria, then soon others would as well. I needed to keep a lid on things and no better way than to make her less available to me during the day.

"On it, boss."

Massimo left and I returned the camera feed to cover the entirety of the estate. When I left, Massimo was laying down the law with Simon, our IT guy and the center of our security system. Time to make myself scarce.

CHAPTER EIGHT

Vittoria

"O Romeo, Romeo, wherefore art thou Romeo?"

Now I knew how Juliet felt when she stood gazing out at the moon wondering why she had to fall for the one guy guaranteed to fuck up her life the most. And yet here I was — pining for his gaze, his knowing touch, and feeling very much the star-crossed lover pining for her Romeo. What the hell was wrong with me? Sure, he had an icy glare and dominant demeanor and could be a complete asshole about obedience, but when the ice turned to a consuming fire, I couldn't get enough of him.

It had been a week since our episode in his office and we hadn't had sex since. I slept in an empty bed most nights or woke to see his retreating back as he left early in the morning.

He must be angry with me, but he hadn't punished me and even my ass was missing the heat that his hand made when he spanked me. How had I become a total slut in such a short time? Mind you, his slut and no one else's, although I wasn't opposed to flirting up a guard in an attempt to win a little help in my eventual escape. I had no intention of going further than a coy glance or giggle, of course, but surely there wasn't any harm in making a friend... or making a friend think he stood a shoot of something more.

Someone must have told him how close I was getting to Theo, because the day after our stroll in the garden, he was gone and replaced with a giant who didn't speak. Typical of Romeo to give me a mute who seemed oblivious to my charms, but I still had Carlo, who didn't say much, but seemed to be a sympathetic listener at least.

On the plus side, Romeo must have felt bad for not seeing me because he'd lifted the ban on me leaving the property. But it wasn't like I was free either. I had four guards with me at all times. I expected as much. After all, my mother and I had been well guarded anytime we went anywhere. After she died, my father doubled my watch, even though my mother's death hadn't been the result of a mafia strike. She'd had a bad reaction to a new medication prescribed by her doctor. My father killed that doctor and the pharmacist who had approved it – a wild over-reaction that had only weakened his standing among the families. Perhaps that was why my guard doubled... but it didn't keep me from escaping when I wanted to.

As a child, it had been easy to imagine myself a little princess locked in a tower against my will. Now here I was, Mrs. Vitale, and still a helpless captive princess. I seriously needed to up my game. How could I gain Romeo's attention and get him back in our bed? Or on the desk, that was just as good. Or against the wall, on the floor, in the shower... pretty much anywhere as long as he ravished me fully and completely as only he could.

Think, Vittoria! Seeing me in little to no clothing seemed to have an effect on him. It was a start.

I went to my closet, digging through all the drawers, and riffling through dresses in search of something he hadn't yet seen me in. There were some nice items, designer expensive, but not slutty enough for what I had in mind. Time for a shopping trip!

Grabbing my phone, I called Carlo. I could have probably just asked my new personal guard, but he would only clear it with Carlo anyway, so I went to the source.

An hour later I was sandwiched in the car with my mute giant on one side and Carlo on the other. Additional security followed in another car behind us. Smart, I guess; one could be a getaway car if the tires were shot out on this one. Morbid, I know, but the realities of my life weren't lost on me.

When we parked in front of Feretti's, my favorite boutique, our detail pulled in behind us. Carlo stayed with me while the others checked the store. When given the clear, I stepped out of the vehicle with Carlo shadowing me so close, I could smell his cologne. Inside the shop, Valentina, the shop owner, came and greeted me with a glass of champagne.

We did the double kiss cheek to cheek. "Welcome, Vittoria! It has been too long."

Valentina had work done since last I saw her. Her lips were so full, they looked to burst if she kissed someone too hard. Is this what I had to look forward to in my future, plastic surgery, lipo and the latest fashions? The image didn't really fit with what the young princess-me had envisioned if I ever escaped that tower — long flowy bohemian dresses with my skin kissed golden by the sun of some distant shore, running barefoot through the sand just for the thrill of running... although once older, I'd added a child or two running beside me, screaming in frightful delight while a smiling man made monster faces as he chased us.

Picturing Romeo as that monster was surprisingly easy, only he was shrouded in darkness while the rest of us were lit by the sun. He could be that man, but first I'd have to let him in, and he'd have to want more than a marriage of convenience.

"Earth to Vittoria. Hello?" Valentina woke me from the sun-dappled forest and the bohemian dress back into the present. "What are you looking for today?"

I slipped my arm through hers and led her to the far side of the store.

"Sexy, slutty, and barely there. Do you have anything?"

She grinned. "I see. You are out to bag someone. Good for you, not that you need any help, Vittoria, you're gorgeous already. But yes, the new Spring collection has arrived and lucky for you, there are a stack of ultra-revealing clubbing dresses included. They've become all the rage and the less material, the better."

"Sounds perfect!"

"Step inside room one, and I'll bring you some selections. Undergarments to match?" she asked knowingly.

"Oh no," I giggled, "not unless they are even more suggestive than the dress."

It was Valentina's turn to giggle. She left, and I sat down with my champagne. From talking with Theo before he left, I'd learned that the family owned a ring of clubs, some legal and some not, but one, in particular, was favored by the Vitale brothers and run personally by Gio, Club Carnage.

I texted the chat room I had with my girlfriends under a false name on Instagram. I'd set it up while in high school so I could make plans with my friends without my father's knowledge. I told them the time and place and put my phone away just as Valentina brought in my selections.

Carlo wouldn't participate in helping me pick out a dress, and Inch, my nickname for my new guard. was as useful as a wet paper bag. In the end, I sent pics to the girls of each outfit until we were down to the top three: a hot pink number that barely covered my ass and had a sizeable cutout on one side, a black mini with spaghetti straps and a plunging neckline, and my personal favorite, a red mini see-through sheath dress with sequins decoratively placed where my boobs, ass crack and vagina were. It also came with a plunging neckline and only a partial back. It had less coverage than my bikini, and that was saying something.

Valentina, getting into the spirit of things, snapped away with my phone while I modeled. In the end, the girls all picked the red one as the winner, but I bought all three with matching lingerie and 6-inch heels.

None of the brothers were at dinner so after complaining of a headache, I excused myself and left the table. Time for a little trouble! I couldn't wait to see Romeo's face when he caught sight of me.

Grabbing a bottle of Amarone della Valpolicella, I escaped to our ensuite and ran the bath. I needed all my bits silky smooth for tonight. At 9 pm, Carlo and Inch showed up to chaperone me and an hour later, we pulled up outside of the club. Carlo escorted me out of the vehicle, and I caught a whiff of his cologne like earlier. I tried to place the familiar scent, but wasn't fast enough to give my brain time to process it.

Carlo left Inch at the entrance by the bar to keep a look out while he brought me over to my girlfriends. As I removed my coat, they all whistled and made playfully crude remarks. I watched Carlo in my periphery, expecting him to ogle me like all the rest of the guys in the club, but that's not what I saw.

A flash of satisfaction that disappeared to be replaced with a blank expression that I almost thought I'd imagined. Could it be that he was actually happy for me to finally get out and have some fun? Well, I could work on discovering how deep Carlo's sympathies ran later. Tonight, I was here for good times and hopefully super sex later on or maybe in the bathroom. I visualized Romeo emptying the bathroom of people and taking me up against the wall.

It surprised me when an hour and four too many ouzos later, I hadn't seen the men yet. Carlo stood guard by my table, watching me closely, almost impatiently. It was like he was waiting for something. Well, he'd been the one ordering our drinks all night, maybe he was waiting for me to pass out, but he had no idea who he was dealing with. I was a Calogerà!

Slamming back two shots, I wobbled onto the dance floor with my girls. The song that was playing was slow and dirty. *Perfecto!* We ground and teased and basically did a show. The floor cleared, leaving us plenty of space, the other patrons being more interested in watching instead of participating with us.

Then I felt it. Prickles along my skin. Someone was watching me, but it wasn't my husband. I searched for the source and at the bar, a man glowered in my direction. Pretending not to notice him, I glanced away and moments later, the prickling sensation left as I lost myself in the dirty song with my bestie, Gia, grinding her ass against mine.

My eyes roamed the club and traveled up to a platform I hadn't noticed before, where several sets of eyes were watching me. Ah, the band of brothers! I knew they'd be here. Gio, Tano, Vinny, Tony, Fausto, and Massimo, and settled on Romeo. His glare traveled down my body, so being the brat I am, I turned around and wiggled my ass in his direction, then spun back around and blew him a kiss.

His glare seared me, sending tingles down my core and zapping my clit. I couldn't look away and neither, it seemed, could he. I danced, not with Gia, although she was there, her body bumping and sliding along mine to the beat of the music. For him. Only for him. We were alone in the club, alone in the world... until a waitress passing the brothers' table paused, following their collective gaze, then slammed her tray down, picked up a glass and poured its contents onto Gaetano's lap.

Romeo leapt up with the rest of his brothers, and the spell his gaze held over me broke, leaving me weak-kneed and gasping. I watched in fascination as the waitress stormed away, with

Gaetano, and Giovani hot on her heels. I returned to my table to have another shot.

"I think you've had enough to drink, Mrs. Vitale." Carlo said gently.

"Says who? My husband? Did he tell you to order me to stop drinking? I think not."

Everything moved in slow motion as my fingers reached for the shot glass.

My girlfriends gasped.

A tanned muscular hand gripped my wrist, his heat burning all the way through my body to my knees.

Romeo.

He tugged me to him and wrapped one arm possessively around me. "Aren't you going to introduce me to your friends, *wife?*"

His embrace didn't fool me for a moment. Anger radiated from him, melting my insides to goo.

My girlfriends' mouths hung open. Then Romeo reached out to Gia, the most promiscuous of our group and gently tugged her closer. Holding her gaze, he dropped a soft, sensual kiss on the back of her hand.

"Hi, I'm Gia. Nice to meet you, Romeo." She wet her mouth with her tongue and bit provocatively on her bottom lip.

Bitch!

Romeo chuckled. "The pleasure is all mine, Gia."

Bastard!

I have seriously underestimated my husband's sexual prowess and tried to pull away, but his arm was like an iron band around my shoulders. One by one, the girls fell to his charm, and I hated him for it. If this was his version of punishment, it was working.

His brothers slowly circled us, all but Tano, presumably cleaning himself up, and Gio, who had gone after the waitress. Suddenly surrounded by handsome men, my friends were tripping over themselves to get at them. Gia's gaze moved from Romeo to Massimo and I saw a flutter of desire pass between them as he held her gaze. I watched fascinated as Gia was held by Massimo's glare, until he broke it by having Fausto, Tony and Vinny take the ladies to the dance floor.

"Make sure they make it home safely, Massimo," Romeo ordered.

"Yes, boss. Anything else?"

"Get the camera footage from Gio and find out who that guy at the bar was, and report back in the morning. I'll need some time to punish my errant wife and don't want to be disturbed." He snapped his fingers at Carlo. "You will be dealt with later." Keeping his steel grip on me, Romeo hustled us from the club with two of his guards clearing the way.

Once in the car and safely buckled in, my arms crossed against my chest, I finally spared a moment to glare at Romeo.

"I hate you!" I pouted.

His eyes glittered dangerously. "So you keep saying. But I think you'll change your tune."

The promise in his eyes was unmistakable. To anyone else, Romeo would appear composed, cold, in full control, but the dark pools devoid of light spoke of another Romeo.

Primal.

A shock skittered down my spine and bloomed in my core. I was in trouble, and I hoped my shenanigans were worth whatever was about to happen.

As usual, Romeo seemed able to read my thoughts. "Don't worry, *Principessa*, you won't be getting the attention of other men again."

Is that what he thought? That I was there to get attention from other men? Shit!

"But Rom —"

"Quiet!" He cut me off, and the harshness in his tone set me on edge.

"But —" I tried again.

Romeo undid my seat belt and hauled me over his lap. His hand came down on my skimpily covered backside. Intense heat erupted where his hand landed. I squirmed, trying to avoid the smacks as they landed so fast and took my breath away.

"What's the matter, wife? Don't like the attention you asked for?"

A flurry of swats continued to land. I cried, great wracking sobs and I was so embarrassed with my husband's guards in the front seats hearing the spanking and me crying.

Ripping the back of the dress over my hips, Romeo continued to spank me until I hung limply over his lap, crying my eyes out, with no energy left to fight him. Heat encased my ass, making the skin feel tight and swollen. All the guys in the front would have to do is turn their heads to see me, my naked ass beet red, a glowing beacon in the darkness.

When the car pulled up, Romeo positioned me in his arms and carried me out of the car and into the house. He stalked down the darkened hallway to our suite, every step felt as if I was getting closer to the guillotine. The excitement of getting his attention wore off, and I was now beset with the realization that I'd fucked up.

CHAPTER NINE

Romeo

"Again."

Massimo swung his fist, connecting with a bloody jaw. The jaw belonged to a guy tied to a chair in one of our warehouses along the docks, where he'd been caught sniffing around one of a dozen identical shipping containers... one that just so happened to be the only one belonging to the Grassiano family.

Another shipment had been stolen off our docks and while the Vitale family had enough money to compensate the offended family, it still made us look weak, like we lacked control over our territory. That would not do, because we'd built our reputation on control.

My father's words came to me when I got the call from Massimo about the missing shipment of cocaine. It was one thing to lose 20 tons of the drug in its raw form, and had it been ours, we may not have had to look as hard, but this shipment was pirated in our shipping lane and was street-ready.

That meant that the motherfuckers made off with about two billion worth of product.

"Your life is already forfeit, but if you want your family to live, you better spill." Massimo's dark nature could be absolutely terrifying and was why he was considered the most formidable enforcer our organization had.

At his threatening words, the guy in the chair pissed himself. He was a low life, but he knew something, and I was more than happy to keep torturing him for days to find out what it was.

"Give me the drill," Massimo asked casually. He reached out a monstrous hand, covered in blood and rings, slowly, making sure that the guy in the chair took note of his size which dwarfed the size of the drill.

"Please," he begged. "I don't know anything."

Unmoved, Massimo turned on the drill. "I can poke holes in you for days before you die." Aiming the drill at the tied man's hand, Massimo took his time lowering the drill, pressing the button to make acceleration sounds as he did.

The rest of our men watched Massimo work with a queasy sort of admiration. Only I knew it for the performance it was. Oh, he could follow through when he had to, but manipulating fear, not pain, was Massimo's real talent. He could only stomach the more physical aspects of this job because he classified it as protecting me. We'd talked a while back, after a particularly gruesome evening, and he'd shared that little nugget with me.

"You're my family, Rom, my brother, and my boss. I would do anything to keep you safe." And that in a nutshell was Simo, a terrifying enforcer on the one side and big protective teddy bear on the other.

He had girlfriends that all ran from him, claiming he was too possessive, too attached to their personal safety and they'd felt suffocated. He told me this and I chuckled at his surprise by this information. He really had no idea how intense he could be, but for one lucky woman maybe one day, he would be the best protector they could have. He liked finding tiny broken things and mending them back to health, funny for a guy who also killed with those same hands, but that was the paradox of Massimo Di Mauro.

As the drill lowered, a hair's breadth from touchdown, the guy finally broke. "Wait! I did see something."

Massimo raised the drill, but kept it on.

"Oh?" he asked, casually brushing sweat-damp strands of hair away from the man's left eye, then framing it with one hand meaningfully. "And what did you see."

"The boss sent me to check on another shipment and there was a group of guys heading out to sea," the man said in a breathless rush, staring at the drill as Massimo lifted it closer to his exposed, wide-open eye "They didn't see me because I was behind them as they pulled out. They headed in the direction of the boat bringing in your shipment. When it didn't arrive, I told my boss what I saw."

"And could you identify any of them?"

Any soldier worth anything could see the lie in the guy's eyes when he said 'yes'. He was just trying to prolong the inevitable.

Massimo straightened, passing off the drill to one of his subordinates.

"End it," I ordered and left the warehouse. The gunshot was barely heard above the horn of an incoming ship. Done with the unsavory business, I wanted to lose myself in Vittoria's soft pliant body until the day disappeared, but I wasn't ready to break that particular seal yet and instead directed our driver to take us to Club Carnage for our regular Friday Night catch-up session even though I hadn't attended the last few, not since getting married. But I needed it tonight, time with them.

At our reserved table, I caught up with Gaetano whom I hadn't seen since the wedding. Our resident surgeon had an apartment near the hospital for when he worked nights. His last shift ended at 6 am this morning, giving him plenty of time to sleep before joining us.

I wanted to discuss his protection detail, but Tano refused to accept that he needed any. Still, I had made sure the best security was installed at his condo, and that there were extra guards at the hospital when he worked.

"Would you look at the ass on that one," Gio remarked.

One by one, we all looked down and were at once captivated by a group of young women, barely dressed for trouble, grinding against each other to the music.

"They are all pretty hot," Vinny added. "Maybe I should go and talk with them."

"Yeah, Vinny," Fausto said dryly, "take one for the team."

"What the hell is Little Red wearing? I swear I can see all the way to Albuquerque when she bends over like that. Holy shit, she works it like a pro. Who are those women, Gio?"

"Don't look at me. I've never seen them before, but one seems kind of familiar."

Almost as if hearing us talk about her, the one in the almost see-through mini-dress looked up. I froze in my chair as her eyes scanned the group until they landed on me.

What the fuck was my wife doing here, and dressed like that!

As if she'd read my thought, she turned around and wiggled her ass at me, then the little minx gazed over her shoulder and blew me a kiss.

The little...!

I closed my hand around my glass to keep from making a fist, but I couldn't drink. I couldn't even think clearly. I wanted to get down there — hell, I wanted to vault over the low wall and rip the eyes out of every man in this room who dared to look at my wife — but I didn't do that either. I was as captive as any other man there, entranced by her movements.

I had no idea how long I just sat there, locked in place by

rage and desire, but then the waitress walked by and saw Gaetano watching the floor show my wife and her friends were giving the entire club.

Glancing away from the waitress. I noticed a group of men at the bar. One, the closest to the floor was watching Vittoria with a kind of fascinated disgust. I didn't like it one bit.

"What the hell is wrong with you?" Tano sprang to his feet, now drenched in his drink and yelling at the waitress who gave him the middle finger. She hustled away from our table with Tano hot on her heels.

My eyes flew to Simo. "What the fuck?"

He shrugged. "Apparently, he knows her."

"Of course he does."

Gio sighed and pushed his chair back. "Come on, boys. Let's divide and conquer. I'll take the high road, you take the low road."

I was barely aware of going downstairs. It seemed I took just a few steps and arrived at Vittoria's table, where she and her friends were arguing with Carlo about another round of shots. As my wife reached defiantly for a drink, I caught her wrist and pulled her away, trapping her under my arm where I could keep her drinking under wraps.

Her girlfriends openly stared at me, their surprise at my sudden appearance drunkenly sliding into appreciation as they looked me over. One of them made a point of licking her lips, some friend! But it gave me an opportunity to give my wife a taste of her own medicine

As I introduced myself to Gia, lingering over the kiss I placed on the back of her hand, I could see a jealous heat in Vittoria's eyes and... a hurt betrayal, just as if she hadn't been shaking her ass at every man in this club. But seeing her hurt sucked the fun out of my revenge. It was time to leave.

At my nod, my brothers whisked the girls off to the dance floor, leaving me and Vittoria alone with Massimo and Carlo. I have no idea what the little fucker was thinking bringing her here, but I planned on showing him just how much I didn't appreciate what he'd done.

"Make sure they make it home safely, Massimo." I said, keeping my eyes on Carlo.

"Yes, boss. Anything else?"

"Get the camera footage from Gio and find out who that guy at the bar was, and report back in the morning. I'll need some time to punish my errant wife and don't want to be disturbed."

Vittoria's cheeks bloomed bright red with indignation and embarrassment. She had no idea how lucky she was that I didn't rip that dress off her and spank her right there. But I had no interest in making a scene at the moment.

"You," I snap at Carlo, "will be dealt with later."

Keeping a firm grip on Vittoria, I hustled us out of the club. At the exit, her bodyguard joined me in escorting us to my vehicle, but he didn't get in the car. Julius was old school, part of my father's guard. He knew his place, unlike that little shit who stood off to the side watching my wife with hungry eyes.

I secured Vittoria's seat belt and climbed in beside her. She's perfectly capable, but it is important she understood the power exchange here. She was no longer in control of the evening. I was.

"I hate you!" she pouts and slams her arms across her chest.

"So you keep saying, but I think you'll change your tune." I allowed my intentions to come through in my tone, while my eyes glittered imparting the impending danger my little brat would soon find herself in.

Her body responded as I knew it would. The scent of her arousal hung in the air between us. If I reached down and slid my finger between her folds, I knew she'd be soaked. Her pupils dilated and her pulse picked up. She liked danger, my girl, and liked paying the price for being naughty.

"Don't worry, *Principessa*, you won't be getting the attention of other men again."

She had the temerity to look confused by that, and my temper got the better of me. The little brat had gone out of her way to get attention, well now she had it. Hope she liked the consequences of baiting me.

"But Rom —"

"Quiet!" I snapped in a tone I usually reserved for men already on their knees to beg my forgiveness.

It had no effect on Vittoria, who continued her stammering efforts to explain herself and her inexcusable behavior.

I was done. Undoing her seatbelt, I tugged her over my lap. Bringing my hand down on her backside, the useless string tucked alluringly between her ass cheeks and the sheer material of her dress did nothing to protect her backside from me.

"What's the matter, wife? Don't like the attention you asked for?"

My men knew better than to turn around or interrupt me. So, I knew when I tugged her dress above her hips and displayed her ass, they wouldn't look. I brought my hand down with ruthless efficiency.

With every crack of my hand on her ass, she cried and begged but I had no interest in being lenient tonight. She had this coming and would learn to swallow her medicine and fall in line.

I didn't stop spanking her until she hung limply over my lap, completely spent. Which happened to be perfectly timed with our arrival home. I tossed my jacket over her and then twisted her as I scooped her up into my arms.

Her make-up was smudged, and dual rows of mascara tracked down each cheek. She wasn't mad any longer and gazed up at me with a rare look of vulnerability. Opening our bedroom door, I didn't waste any time setting the scene for her punishment.

I placed her at the base of the bed and lay her on her back. Taking one long leg, I wrapped a soft fur-lined cuff around her ankle and clipped it to the chain that hung down the bed post. Then I did her other leg and with them fully extended and parted as wide as they could go, there was no hiding anything from me.

I did her wrists next, almost disappointed when Vittoria didn't put up a fight. I grabbed a fuck-machine from my closet and set it up at the end of the bed on a bench. Turning on the machine, I tested the distance from the tip of the dildo to her entrance. I wanted to make sure her labia would be penetrated but not overly stimulate her clit. This would be a slow burn, a building of excitement until she was so desperate, she would beg for release.

Vittoria had lifted her head to see what I was doing and when she saw the fuck-machine, her eyes grew wide.

"Don't worry. You will barely feel it. But it will become like an itch that no matter what you do, you can't scratch. This is a lesson in what happens when you go out in public almost naked and air-fuck your friends in front of complete strangers."

I left her there to marinate in anticipation and went to the kitchen, where I peeled a nice-sized piece of ginger for her tight little back hole. I waited another ten minutes and returned to the room. Vittoria was doing her best to shift her hips closer to the dildo, but her legs were firmly held in place and no matter what she did, she couldn't get closer.

"What's the matter, my *principessa*? Were you hoping to get yourself a little penetration?

Her weeping pussy dripped down to her anus. I swirled the ginger through it to coat it in her natural lubricant, then pushed the ginger in her back hole until it was fully seated inside of her.

Standing back, I had to admire the sight she made.

Fucking gorgeous! The bottom of her reddened ass cheeks were in the air, with the handle of the root standing out. The dildo moved with a constant precision designed to stimulate, but not satisfy her.

The moment the heat from the ginger kicked in, she yelped with surprise.

"What is that? Romeo, it's... it's hot! Get it out!"

"No. I will not take it out. Not until I feel you've learned your lesson." I jostled the root plug, short thrusts to encourage a fresh flow of juice.

She moaned, thrashing from side to side as if that could help her escape the heat building inside of her.

"Please, Romeo, please fuck me! The burn, it's driving me insane!"

"As intended. I'll be back soon to check on you."

"You son of a bitch!" she yelled from the bed. "Get back here, Romeo!"

I took the secret passage to my office, opened my phone and texted Massimo. "Were the women taken home?"

"Yes. Dealt with."

One less headache at least.

"Where is Carlo?"

I was furious the shithead had taken such liberties as to not communicate with Massimo, his boss, beyond stating she was meeting with some girlfriends. Had my wife secured herself an ally for herself in my household?

"In one of the holding rooms awaiting his punishment."

"Meet me there at 8 am."

"Understood. Good night."

Time for phase two. I stalked back to the bedroom. She must have heard me enter the room as she lifted her head and held my gaze. There was no trace of anger in her now, but even the desire I saw couldn't hide the edge of animosity brewing in her beautiful eyes.

"Did you want me to film and send this to the host of men watching you this evening?" I asked coolly. I never would, but she didn't know me well enough yet to know that. "I'm sure Gio could provide me with a list of names."

She hesitated as a pink flush born of embarrassment and need spread across her beautiful body. "It's not what you think, Romeo."

Sure, I'd play. "Oh? And what am I thinking?"

She dropped her eyes and chewed her lower lip. She was either working up to a great lie, or an honest confession.

"You thought I wanted to show off and get everyone's attention? But that's not true."

She paused. Here it came... truth or more lies?

"I wanted you to notice me."

I chuckled darkly. "Explain."

"You've been ignoring me since that evening in your office. I wanted you to see me."

A tear threatened to fall, but she quickly blinked it away. See her? How could I not see her? She was in my head every waking minute of the day.

"You cooked up this elaborate scheme to get your own husband's attention?"

"Yes."

"Why?"

Her expressions morphed so quickly from one to the next with my question, I wasn't sure I'd witnessed the plethora of her feelings in her expressive eyes until she closed off completely. A slight glare replaced the desperation from a moment ago.

"I asked you a question. Answer me." I was a bit of a twisted shit, I admit it, but I wanted to hear the words come out of her mouth.

"It should be obvious," she pouted. She was so cute, with her legs hiked in the air and her arms extended, pulling off such an innocent pout.

Vittoria never ceased to impress me with her strength and

character. But I wasn't here to admire my wife. I was here to punish the thoughtless little girl she behaved like. Once again, she'd acted without thinking, tried to seize my attention by flaunting herself in a crowded club.

"You should know, I've peeled plenty of ginger and can replace the one in your ass whenever you need a fresh piece to squeeze."

Her eyes narrowed. But not before her pupils dilated. She didn't hate her torture as much as she let on, but didn't want me to know that.

"Have it your way," I said and left her to think over her predicament while I grabbed a fresh piece of ginger from the kitchen.

Back in the bedroom, I removed the fuck-machine and raised the notch on the ankles cuff attachment, so her weight moved from her mid-back to her shoulders. Now she had plenty to say, but the time for apologies was over.

The new ginger drove a fresh heat wave through her. A glossy sheen covered her body, especially her inner thighs, shiny with her excitement. Fresh ginger juice trickled between her puffy lips, mingling with her oils and following gravity to drip onto her belly.

She was perfect and mine! The belt slithered through the loops making a shhhh-ing sound that alerted my pretty captive to what was coming next. I'd learned that my princess was especially sensitive to leather.

Her head tilted up and showed the slits of her eyes and the desire swirling in their pretty depths.

"I have what you need, baby girl, just admit it's me you want."

I lashed her trembling flesh, right across the handle of the ginger.

A sobbing moan shivered from my wife's lips and I could see her slick opening quiver, cramping with need.

She's perfect. A blend of brat and goddess, in control and no control, hungry pain-slut and submissive little girl. But she was still holding back and I needed to break through the barrier and get inside her secret. Smash it and take the burden from her. Carry it or destroy it, whatever was fitting.

Thwack! The leather striped her backside just above the plug and close to her sweet pouty nether lips. She wailed and sobbed. Her inner thighs were drenched with her sweet nectar. So sweet, I was having a hard time holding back.

Up and down her backside, I painted her pale flesh rosy pink. When I reached her sit spot and moved the strokes to her thighs. Vittoria howled, her body tensing as a powerful orgasm overtook her.

What the hell? I knew my princess liked her pleasure spiked with pain, but I hadn't realized she could reach climax just from a spanking. Of all the women I'd known who enjoyed playing such games with me, that was a first.

"Romeo, please, I need you," she cried when her body relaxed.

"Say the words I want to hear, Vittoria," I prompted, ready to deliver her reward for saying she was mine and only mine.

"I love you," she whispered.

Soft words, so quiet in contrast to the pounding of my heart, which was so loud that surely she could hear it too. How could she love me? This wasn't supposed to happen, yet...

Yet something inside of me responded. I loved her too. The realization was shocking and held me motionless at the foot of the massive bed.

I loved my wife. When did that happen? How? I dropped the belt and yanked out the plug. Toeing off my shoes and shucking my pants and boxers in record time, I lined myself up with her entrance.

"Your wish is my command, *Principessa.*" Slamming my hips forward, her tight slickness enveloped me and pulled me in deep. Her body welcomed my invasion and begged to be conquered.

"Vittoria," I moaned, my balls slapping her fiery ass.

"*Romeooo!*" she screamed, convulsing around my cock, milking me to a powerful orgasm. A low growly moan escaped me as I emptied into her spasming pussy. I almost passed out on top of her, but I kept my legs beneath me and pulled my half-hard cock from her.

Slowly, I uncuffed her ankles and massaged her legs before moving to her wrists. She was still, spent and either asleep as I moved through these tasks or floating in the aftershocks. But when I came to wipe between her legs, her eyes fluttered open and gazed into mine.

There was still a secret swimming in those sparkling eyes, but whatever resistance that had been there since she fell into my arms on her father's property was gone. After wiping myself down and removing my shirt. I climbed on the bed and covered us, pulling her into my arms, her very warm backside snuggled against my crotch.

My cock liked feeling her punished bottom and slowly grew, pressing between her scalded cheeks and that was how I woke up the next morning. Quietly, I dressed and went down to the business level of my home to meet Massimo and decide how to best deal with Carlo.

CHAPTER TEN

Vittoria

Oh god, why am I so sore? I was slow to awaken, even slower to clear my heavy head and find my memories. Last night... I'd told him I loved him. *Why?*

My process had turned complicated and last night's confession was proof of that. I needed to get myself under control and out from under his. How was I supposed to leave a man I apparently was in love with?

I needed to calm the hell down and get my raging hormones in check. I rolled onto my back, knowing I was alone before reaching out and feeling the cool sheets on his side of the bed. He'd left a while ago. Good. Or, maybe not so good. I was so confused, upset he wasn't there and relieved at the same time.

Groaning, I rolled onto my tummy. My ass throbbed inside and out, and so did my poor little kitty. Everything felt deliciously used and abused. Bending my knees, I slid my hand down my flat belly and between my legs. Just thinking about last night had me wet and wanting.

My body was still in a heightened state after last night's edging torture. Why couldn't he have punished me with forced orgasms instead? Because he knew I'd prefer it, of course. And he knew I'd still be suffering the effects of withheld pleasure this morning. I needed release and I needed it now!

I wanted a vibrator and now knew just where to look. Rolling to my feet, I took a quick trip to the bathroom to relieve my bladder and then went to the walk-in. Snooping the other day had turned up an entire collection of naughty toys, most of which were still in the packaging.

Had he bought them to use on me... or had he bought them to use on someone else before me? The idea woke jealousy like a snake to wind through me, coiling tight and biting deep.

"Ugh! Get a grip, Vittoria," I uttered aloud in the empty room. Opening the cupboard under his accessory drawers, I dug through until I found a double vibrator. The long end would hit my pleasure center and the second one would tickle the entrance of my anus. Yum!

I ripped it out of the packaging and washed it thoroughly in the bathroom sink before rushing to bed. My urgency surprised me. I'd never felt the need to masturbate, mostly because my previous sexual experiences had been so bland that I believed the female orgasm must be a myth. Since Romeo had proven otherwise so often and so intensely, I was horny all the damn time.

I felt wicked lying on my back, parting my legs wide. Hadn't he told me many times that my pleasure belonged to him? But he'd never expressly told me I couldn't relieve myself. And why have all those toys if not for my pleasure?

I tried various speeds before getting comfortable and finally, the damn device sprang to life! I slid a hand over one breast and gripped the needy bud. Even my nipples hurt, yearning for sexual release.

With my free hand, I slid the vibrator inside until the

slightly shorter side pressed inside the opening of my ass. "*Yes,*" I hissed in the silent bedroom. I was so turned on I treated the bud roughly, pinching and rolling it in my best imitation of Romeo's expert touch.

"Ahhhh!" I cried out as a powerful wave kicked through me of the edge and sent my libido sprawling into pleasure-space where I rode the wave that gripped me. I lay panting from the exertion deciding if I wanted a second go when the door opened.

"What have we here? A naughty little girl playing with Daddy's toy without permission?"

Oh shit, why did his warning send waves of desire through me? "I — er — uhmm..."

Crap, this was so embarrassing.

"Cat got your tongue?" He closed the distance between us in long, swift strides. Leaning over me beside the bed, he planted his fists on either side of my shoulders, caging me under him.

Drawing up a knee, he pressed it against my soaking petals. I was sure he'd have a wet stain there when he pulled it away. "What did I tell you about this little kitty, wife? Hmm?"

"That it belongs to you?"

"That's right. And did you ask my permission to touch my pussy?"

"Well, no, but it wasn't listening to me either," I pouted. "I told it to calm the hell down, but, well, it just got more demanding. Not my fault."

Romeo, who hadn't looked upset at all, broke out in laughter. I was so shocked by his response, my jaw dropped, which just seemed to rile him up even more.

"Why are you laughing?" I demanded.

He calmed down, although the merriment remained in the gold of his eyes. Note to self: when he's angry, the amber goes dark, almost black. When he's hungry, they do darken, but when he's teasing or happy, they turn amber gold. But more gold than anything.

I liked it, almost as much as the darkness that swirls through him. Romeo was dangerous, a predator, but he was also a man, my man, and for the first time, I was able to separate the Dom from the Don.

"I was just wondering if this is how you learned to get your own way growing up? You seem to think all you have to do is stomp your little princess foot, cross your arms and stick out your lip, and I'll give you anything you want. Why, you're not Donna Vittoria at all, you're a child!"

Oh, no! That was as close to seeing my other part as I wanted him to see. My little princess is locked tightly away in a tower in a faraway land. No one had ever entered the tower and I wasn't about to fling the doors wide open and invite in a love that couldn't exist between us. If he knew how submissive I truly was, how I craved his strength and guidance, I'd be sunk! Just like the fairy tale, I wanted a handsome prince on his noble steed to come and rescue me. If anyone could play the part of the handsome knight, it was Romeo, but there was no shining armor, only darkness. If he knew what I truly desired, he would make a mockery of it and my dreams would die.

His cock was a magic wand that I couldn't get enough of and my moment of weakness when I uttered those three powerful words, *I love you...* that changed everything between us. Or it could have, except he didn't say it back.

I slammed the door to my heart and gazed at him with my façade back in place. Men like Romeo didn't cherish. They broke their toys, just like my father did to my mother. I couldn't allow myself to become yet another mafia victim. I needed to stay strong and rely on myself and then one day, maybe, I would be free to pursue a man that could fully love me.

I don't know why the struggle was so real. I'd known for years now that my father would eventually find a way to pawn me on a dangerous man, someone who wanted a woman to run his household and bear his children, not because he loved me, but because he could shore up my father's flagging power.

The reality was not so far off from what I'd anticipated. I was taken from my home and brought to someone else's and forced to marry a man I didn't know. But nothing else was as I thought it would be. He didn't demand I run his household; he had his mother for that. She didn't push me either, just made herself available to me when I wanted to learn. I had been cuffed to the bed and denied any unsupervised access to the outside world, but I'd also been welcomed as one of the family. True, my welcome varied from person to person; Massimo and I steered clear of each other as much as we could, but his other brothers so far had been fun and kind to me, and his mother seemed to accept me with all the warmth she might have had for her own daughter. The staff might have been indifferent to my pleas for escape, but they were respectful and attentive toward me. Even my dreaded security guards...

Well, not all of them were dreadful.

"What happened to Carlo?" I asked.

His eye color changed. I watched in fascination as the gold darkened to amber but didn't stop until they reached a rich brown. I guess that question had been a mistake.

"Carlo isn't your concern," he said curtly.

I was about to reply that it was so when his lips crashed against mine. Romeo's tongue pushed past my lips and tangled with mine.

"Mmm." I moaned into his mouth. If this was his way of shutting me up, then I'd have to speak out of turn more often!

Leaning on one arm, Romeo undid his fly and pulled his engorged cock out of its confines. Pressing my knees to my ears, he entered me in one powerful thrust of his hips.

Opening my eyes, I found him watching me, devouring me with his eyes, while he pinned me with his demanding cock. His eyes had shifted again to show me the color of his desire — light again, rich not with gold but with reddish highlights. Like a demon's eyes, I thought, and shivered as I embraced him. The Devil in him, riding me.

He placed my leg over his shoulder, deepening his thrusts when I whimpered.

"You are mine, *Principessa,* and you do not think about other men, ever!"

He brought up my other leg and drove himself inside me, so deep I felt certain he'd split me in half. Was he going to fuck me to death? His Devil's eyes never left mine as he fucked me within an inch of my life.

"You!" *Thrust* "Belong!" *Thrust* "To *me*!"

His last word swept up to a roar, followed by the hot bloom of his cum filling me, setting off my own orgasm. As I cried out in the grip of my pleasure, my body seized on his, forcing me to fully experience even the smallest sensation as he pumped his heat inside me.

Sex with Romeo was always a primal thing, but now I felt it too, that animalistic pleasure that came not from fucking, but being fucked. Claimed by my mate. Marked with his seed. And all at once, I felt very silly for ever thinking I could defy this man, my Master. I was his. No matter how far I ran or where I hid, he would track me down, because I was his... and I wanted to be his. My body was too wrung from pleasure to move, but my heart raced with something like panic.

Suddenly, Romeo rolled onto the floor and took me with him, holding me atop him. Sunshine splashed over us from the open curtains, bathing us in warmth.

"It's a beautiful day," he said as if reading my mind. "Would you like to go out?"

I craned my neck to look back at him. "With you? I thought you had to work?"

A little gold shone in the inky depths, warmth, like the sun warming me with his gaze. Surrounded by the sun as we were, he reminded me of a lion. "Yes, with me. I think my girl needs some attention, and I would rather it be positive, so you earn yourself a good girl spanking."

His hand slid down my back and gripped one of my battered cheeks, kneading it until I yelped. "But first, you must be punished for taking that orgasm from me."

"Will I like this punishment?"

"We'll see." He smirked, tugging me to my feet. "Let's go, kitten, we need to clean you up."

* * *

An hour later and another blow job later, we left the apartment dressed casually for our date. I had no idea what to expect, but I looked forward to it. Being out with Romeo for the first time in a social setting really shone a light on the circumstances of our marriage.

Could it even be valid if it's performed against someone's will? Maybe not for most people, but I wasn't most people. I was the only child of Santo Calogerà, a daughter born with a duty, just as Romeo had performed his duty as a son of Luciano Vitale to take a wife, not for love, but for power. That was the reality of our world. Did he want out as badly as I did? Somewhere, were there lovers begging for his attention? Or a mistress who had his heart, but who his family found unsuitable for marriage, someone I would eventually be required to meet and perhaps even befriend? Or did he prefer sex to be transactional, uncomplicated by emotion, serviced by professionals on reserve?

I know he was as surprised as I was that we were so compatible sexually. But mentally, and emotionally, could we ever be as naturally aligned as we were in the sack?

"Where are we going?" I asked.

"No questions, *Principessa*. You'll see when we get there."

I was surprised when Romeo took me to the garage and told me to get in a sexy black sports car. "No guards?"

"Yes, guards, but not here with us."

He helped me in and buckled my seat belt. Oh, I loved this tame version of my monster, the one where he held doors and treated me as a lady. As long as it wasn't a shift in the power exchange between us, because I really enjoyed my dark nasty monster.

The car roared to life, and we zipped down the driveway to the gate and out onto the main road. I leaned back, a smile on my face. No matter what happened now, I somehow knew the day would be a good one.

An hour later we were sitting on a rooftop near the water-front sipping mojitos. Not having had breakfast, the drink went right to my head but took care of the remnant of the hangover I'd woken up with.

The deck was surrounded by beautiful flowering vines, offering each guest privacy from their neighbor. Not that we had many to begin with, as there were only two other tables with guests and they were on the far side.

"This is a pretty spot. Thank you for bringing me."

He lifted his glass and clinked mine. "To us," he toasted.

"To us."

When the food arrived, Romeo fed me a bite of each item before allowing me to eat by myself, reminiscent of our wedding day.

"The food is delicious. Why isn't the place busier?" I asked before allowing an oyster to slip down my throat.

"It usually is, but it's a family venue and I bought it out for our luncheon. Those tables are taken up with our guards."

"They are?" How had I not noticed? He was right when he said we would be guarded, yet have privacy. But wait, a family venue? "Does that mean Vincenzo is here?"

"I'm sure he's somewhere around here looking for ego strokes."

"You do me a disservice, brother!" Vinny's handsome face popped around the floral arboretum. I couldn't help but laugh. He was the exact opposite to his brother. Where Romeo was all dark and swarthy and often closed off, Vincenzo was light, care-free and completely in the moment every time I saw him, which hadn't been often, but I was looking forward to getting to know this brother who followed his dreams.

"Sister!" he cried, gently taking my hand and kissing the back.

"Watch it!" Romeo growled.

Vinny smiled, his eyes sliding to me. "How did you manage to get my grumpy brother to take an afternoon off and relax? You must teach me your Jedi ways."

Considering how effortlessly Romeo made me bend to his will, I couldn't help but laugh at that, then huffed, pretending to take offense. "I'll have you know, this was all his idea. Now don't ruin it, Vincenzo," I scolded, "I'm having a wonderful time with my husband."

Romeo perked up at that and smirked at his brother. "You heard her, bugger off."

Shaking his head and muttering in Italian about ungrateful family members, Vinny left us.

"To a peaceful meal." I held up my glass.

My husband smiled. "I'll cheer to that," he said and clinked my glass.

When the meal was done, and the dishes cleared, he patted his lap invitingly. I looked around, ensuring his guards were far enough away not to hear anything that may happen.

"What are you worried about? They heard you less than twenty-four hours ago getting a spanking."

My face went hot. "Thanks for reminding me."

"Now, Vittoria, or they will hear you getting another one."

He'd undone his pants and turned me around, sitting me down on his jutting cock.

The invasion was so sudden, I hissed through gritted teeth as my body took in its massive size, but Romeo didn't give me time to adjust.

He slid his hands under my blouse, freeing the nipples of the lacy bra I wore. He tugged and twisted just the way I liked it as he moved me on him, lifting me easily only to slam me down on his cock, impaling me over and over. My orgasm was so fast, I didn't have time to prepare as heat spiked down my spine, turning my insides molten. I gripped his arms, my hips rolling and bucking helplessly until he swelled inside of me. He tightened his hold on my hips as he filled me with his cum.

"Good girl," he cooed in my ear. He released my breasts and gently tucked them away. He smoothed my shirt but kept me on his lap until his cock softened enough to tuck it back inside.

"Was that dessert?" I teased.

"Why, did you want more?"

"I always want more, Romeo."

Standing, he adjusted his clothing and then took my hand. "Let's go, my insatiable *zoccola*."

"Slut? Really, Romeo, that's not very romantic."

"It may not be romantic, Vittoria, but it is the truth. You are my little slut. Mine to take whenever I want."

He had me there. The ride home was quiet and I was content to watch his muscles clench and relax while he drove, dreaming of his thick digits filling my ass while he took me from behind.

When we pulled up, Massimo was out front pacing like an angry badger. So much for an evening of pleasure. Romeo's entire visage shifted from relaxed to cold control – the Don replacing my Dom. I got out of the car.

"Thank you for the date." I kissed him gently on the cheek,

but before I could leave, he grabbed my arm and tugged me close.

"This isn't over, *zoccola*," he growled in my ear, "only a postponement until later."

He smacked my ass when I turned to leave him with his brother. My heart was feeling full for the first time since I was little and I wasn't at all sure what to do with all of those big feelings. Perhaps having some time alone was just what I needed.

Well, 'alone' was a bit premature. Inch opened the door for me and followed me as I made my way through the house on rubbery legs, but I was too tired and splendidly spent to argue about the need for my security escort here at home. I left my hulking goon on the other side of my suite's door and relaxed on the bed, happy to be alone to think.

CHAPTER ELEVEN

Romeo

"Why am I here?" I asked, leaving the word 'again' hang loudly unspoken in the air. 'Here' was the east-side docks, and despite my question, I knew why. We'd had issues these past few months with our ports and shipping. Ever since the wedding, in fact.

I tried not to think about it too much, but Massimo was like a dog on a bone and would not let go of the idea that somehow Vittoria was responsible.

"We got someone in the back who was sneaking around and thought you'd want to be here in case you had questions."

Fair enough. "Fine, let's go."

Massimo filled me in on the guy they captured while I followed the sounds of a beat-down to the back office. I glanced around at the men watching one of their own tenderize the bleeding man tied to a chair. I recognized my brother, Fausto, and some of his men, and Dante, of course, methodically and expressionlessly working the defenseless bastard's pain centers with a precision Gaetano would envy. The rest were less familiar, but they were all Massimo's personal men, those he'd handpicked and trusted with his life. That alone told me more about the severity of what was going on than the guy in the chair.

Lately, I'd been playing the defense game with all the attacks on our shipments, but I was tired of it and it didn't suit me. I'd decided that morning after leaving my wife with a thoroughly reddened bottom and cum dripping down her inner thighs, that I needed to get ahead of the situation.

Ever since that night at the club, we'd been getting to know each other more. I knew how Massimo felt about my wife's distracting influence, and I had to admit, between satiating her and handling work issues, my dance card had been too full for a heart-to-heart with Simo, but it looked like I needed to and today would be the day.

"Enough." I motioned Dante back and stalked to the chair. Leaning down, I forced his swollen eyes open and made sure he saw me, my face and the steel of my nerve. "Do you know who I am?"

He licked his parched lips. "Yes. Mr. Vitale."

"And you are?"

"Peter, Sir."

"Well, Peter, "I said, "this is how this is going to go. Dante here is going to beat you until you die, and that's just a fact, but he can do that a lot of different ways. For example, he can go slowly, using techniques to keep you on the edge of death for days. You'll feel every slice, every ounce of pain from the nails pried from your fingers, the pinch of the bolt cutters when we start on the joints, the heat from the blowtorch... well, you get the idea. The only one here who can save you from that is me. I suggest you fall in line and tell me what I want to know."

Peter licked his chapped lips and tried to stare me down.

I stepped back. "Dante, if you please."

Peter started fighting, trying to resist the inevitable, but

Dante slammed his own huge hand over Peter's, pinning it to the arm of the chair, and with one swift, efficient yank, the man's right index fingernail was gone.

"I'm going to give you a moment," I said, pulling over a chair to sit facing Peter, out of Dante's way. "Because I want you to think about this, Peter, I really do. I want you to make the right decision —"

Another fingernail, another scream.

"— while I'm still in a listening mood," I continued. "Because I do have other things to do tonight, Peter, and when I decide to go do those things and give up on you, I'm not going to kill you first. I'm going to tell Dante to take his time, make it last as long as possible. I think the record is eight days."

"Ten," Dante grunted and tore out another fingernail.

"I'm a spy!" the guy screamed.

Dante looked at me quizzically and stepped back at my nod.

Peter sagged against his bonds, gasping for breath, blood dripping onto the concrete floor from the tips of his mutilated fingers. "I was sent... to spy on your operation... and report back."

That was almost too easy, considering how well the guy had held up under Dante's fists. "To whom?"

"I only know his first name. Ardo. I've never met the guy. He leaves his instructions on a voicemail, but it's not really his voice, it sounds like a machine. The money magically appears at my doorstep. The guy's a ghost, I swear."

"I don't believe in ghosts." I nodded to Dante and seconds later, two more bloody fingernails lay in a neat row on the table, but I stopped him before he moved onto the other hand.

I studied the man before me, sobbing and drooling blood and still trying to convince me he didn't know anything. Using not only whole words but whole sentences, where other men in his position might be reduced to mindless, broken begging.

"I don't think the fingernails are working," I said and nodded at Dante's toolbox. "Start on the knuckles."

"Wait! I'm supposed to report to him. Maybe…" Peter licked his bloody lips. "Maybe you can track his location."

Massimo went over to take the guy's phone from one of his men, and even from this distance, I could see it wasn't the usual cheap burner. "Is this your personal phone or did he give it to you?" Massimo asked.

Peter spat blood and sagged again, seemingly too dazed to answer.

I held out my hand, but Massimo didn't give me the phone. "What's the unlock code?" he asked.

Peter lifted his head and looked me in the eyes. "I'll only tell him."

Massimo and I exchanged a swift glance as everything wrong with this interrogation suddenly clicked, and then he threw the phone and we were all running out of the warehouse. Over the sound of my brother shouting for backup, I could hear tires screeching outside.

"We've got company. Try and leave one alive," I yell. Just then the warehouse shook from the force of a muffled explosion and the roof fell in. A bomb, probably in his damn cell phone, the one he was trying so hard to get me to hold. This is a fucking clusterfuck!

Behind us, the warehouse was on fire. Massimo's men were quickly lost in the smoke, some stumbling deeper inside, screaming as the flames consumed them. Outside, survivors were being gunned down as they staggered out of the building, choking and blinded by smoke.

I grabbed Massimo, Dante and a handful of others and headed back the way we'd fled, around the flames and out the back, where I found Fausto and a few men firing back on our ambushers.

"Do we know them?" I demand, sliding into cover behind some shipping crates.

Fausto took aim and fired. He was not a good gunman in the way our world thought of them, but at times like this, there was no one I'd rather have with me in a gunfight. He might be slow, but he was accurate, and every time he pulled the trigger, one of the enemy went down for good. "No idea, but —" Another shot; another dead man tumbling off the dock into the water. I leaned out to provide a covering spray of bullets while he calmly reloaded. "— but they sure know us."

"I want one alive to question, Fausto," I ordered and moved beside Massimo.

"It was a set up," he said darkly.

"You don't say."

"I'm sorry, Romeo, I let you down."

"Keep your head in the battle, Simo. we can talk later about your failures. Now, wound one and kill the rest."

Sirens already, dim but getting closer every second. Time to get the hell out of here.

The enemy hadn't quite managed to get the drop on us. Now, between the spreading fire, our counter-attack, and the approaching sirens, they broke and bolted. Both my brothers seized the opportunity – Massimo peppering one guy's legs with bullets and Fausto taking deliberate aim and blasting out another guy's knees, first one and then the other. While the rest of his men grabbed the wounded and got away, Massimo heaved his screaming victim into the trunk of his car and turned to me.

"Go," I ordered. "I'll finish up here!"

Massimo nodded and was gone. Dante seized Fausto's wounded and ran for another car. The rest of our men grabbed their injured and made their getaway in the growing chaos as Fausto and I rallied our surviving troops.

The wind was strong, whipping the flames higher and sending sparks out to other warehouses. I'd lose the whole block for certain, but I didn't care. It would take all night to put the fire out, and although I knew the bullets would be found in an investigation, we paid the authorities well to overlook them. Fausto and I ran to the front of the building in time to see an unfamiliar car, but it had no plates and whoever was behind the tinted windows shot the men attempting to climb in for safety and peeled out. I emptied my gun as they raced away and Fausto fired what should have been a clean head-shot into the driver's window, but either they had bullet-proof windows or there was a ghost behind the wheel.

The guy's a ghost, I swear.

Well, no time to think about it now. Time to get home and gather the family.

Hours, and two slow deaths later, I was no closer to learning who was after me. The men we took talked plenty, but knew nothing. Hired guns, didn't even know who they were shooting at. But even that told me something: that whoever ordered the hit didn't want me to know it was them, and that meant I knew them. At the very least, we had a leak, and possibly more than one.

I hadn't known that, but I wasn't surprised. The thefts and attacks were too perfectly timed. There was no other way for them to know unless they were getting their information from the source. And again, Massimo was quick to point out that those attacks only started after my marriage.

"Vittoria has no part of this," I said in a tone that should have put an end to it, but my brother's frustration was at its limit.

"Why is it so hard for you to accept the obvious fact that Vittoria is a plant, sent here by her father to bring down our organization?"

"I'm getting tired of this, Massimo. Let me ask you, how do you expect Vittoria to have access to this information? She isn't privy to anything we do. The first time our shipments were seized, she was still spending her down-time handcuffed to the bed. I agree the timing is suspicious, but my wife has nothing to do with these attacks. If you had half as much interest in finding the real enemy as you do in blaming her, we'd have them by now."

Massimo scowled, but did seem to take a mental step back and think about it.

"What about her guards?" I prompted. "Do we know where Theo is tonight?"

Massimo shot me another glare. "Yes, he was at the docks, and if he wanted you dead, he'd have put a bullet in you instead of taking three of them making sure you survived. I vetted that man. I trust him."

"We got some new faces around the grounds. You trust all of them like you do Theo?"

"Of course not," Massimo snapped. "Which is why they don't have access to areas with sensitive information! In fact, the only men with that kind of access are yours, mine and —"

"Don't even say it," I warned.

"Look, Rom, we knew things would be shaky after your father died. We knew you expanding the shipping routes would encourage attacks, but these are very targeted and time specific. No one just gets lucky that many times in a row. There has to be an informant in our ranks, high in the ranks."

He was right of course, but what to do...

"Let's get them at their own game," I decided. "We'll plant a dummy schedule that only the senior capos have access to. When they attack, we'll have narrowed down the options. Put trackers on all their vehicles, but don't let them know. And I mean all of them, even what they drive here, is that clear? Let the asshole come to us."

My *consigliere* nodded his head.

"And add Simon to that list," I said. "He has more access than the average soldier and works alone. He could easily share information without getting noticed."

"Consider it done. But, boss —"

"No. I don't want to hear it. Stop stressing about shit and do your job, Massimo. When everything is done and we're back in control, then you can get all maudlin and apologize, but right now, I need your A-game." My tone softened and I gripped his shoulder. "Let it go, brother."

I felt the shift in my brother, his resolve strengthened. He nodded once, silent, and left.

With things under control for the moment, it was time to clean up and eat. I headed for my suite, exhaustion weighing my limbs until each step felt like walking through peanut butter.

Vittoria was waiting for me, wearing nothing but slinky white lingerie. She took one look and jumped to her feet. "Are you okay? What happened?"

"You haven't heard?"

"No, I spent the afternoon in the kitchen with your mother and nonna. I've been here ever since."

Massimo's words from a few days ago played in my head.

"Maybe we underestimated Calogerà. Maybe he's using his daughter to bring down our empire and your wedding was nothing but a ruse."

"Some trouble at the dock, nothing major. I am hungry for food and you."

The comment hung between us.

"Why don't you shower," she suggested, looking troubled. "I'll fetch us some food from the kitchen. Okay? I'll be right back."

She grabbed her robe and was gone. I undressed and stood under the hot water until the blood and stress swirled at my feet and disappeared down the drain.

CHAPTER TWELVE

Vittoria

Sometimes I questioned my tastes. And right now was one of those times. I was out shopping with Gia, Elena, Neomi and Arianna. It was my first time seeing them since the club a few weeks ago. I had been grounded from seeing them for two weeks and not allowed out without my husband to chaperone.

Although Romeo hadn't said anything to me, I felt a change in him after the warehouse explosion. He didn't talk about it, but others did and I overheard enough to come to my own conclusions. Someone had infiltrated his ranks and was causing some serious issues. Soldiers died, his men taken out by an enemy, and even though that was expected in our way of life, it didn't make it any easier.

My detail doubled with a new head of security, Leo. He was older than Carlo had been, closer to my husband's age, but he seemed to know his stuff. Certainly, he knew how to shadow someone. He was always right behind me, but unlike my usual hulking goons, he was so quiet and discreet, I sometimes forgot he was there at all. Right now, Leo was just outside the dressing room where the girls and I went through stacks of designer clothes that none of us needed.

"Your new guard is sexy," Gia purred.

Yeah, seriously questioning my tastes in friends!

"Leo? Or Julius?"

I knew it wasn't Julius, no one thought he was hot. He was a silent giant whose eyes followed me everywhere, his expression never changing. It wasn't that his looks were unattractive, but his entire vibe was off-putting.

"Duh. Leo, of course. Is he, you know, attached?"

Neomi rolled her eyes at me. "Seriously, Gia, does it matter? You fuck them and dump them so quickly, why bother to find out what his status is?"

We giggled when Gia took on a defensive stance. "Some kind of friends you are." She pouted and crossed her arms, earning more laughter from us.

I tried on another dress, staring into my reflection as I imagined Romeo tearing it off me, and oblivious to Gia until she suddenly demanded, "Well?"

"Well, what?" I asked. I kept my eyes wide and innocent, but I knew exactly what she was asking me.

"Ugh! You're impossible." She stomped her Louis Vuitton-clad foot down on the plush rug which swallowed any sound she'd been attempting to make. We broke out in peals of laughter and, after a grudging smile, Gia joined in.

"I need more champagne," she decided "Be right back."

Of course, she went straight to Leo, whose duties did not usually include fetching drinks. We listened in as she flirted with Leo, who seemed not the slightest bit interested in being anything beyond professional and polite.

"Is she for real?" Elena commented. "Why can't she just stick to the websites like a normal person?"

Neomi burst out laughing. "Since when is online dating the new norm?"

"Who said anything about dating?" Elena shot back.

Neomi thought that over. "Well, that's true."

"What's so funny?" Gia asked. Her hands full of champagne flutes and a bottle of bubbly. "Are you going to help me or what?"

"What," I blurted.

Elena and Neomi keeled over with laughter.

"Seriously, how old are you?" Gia chided.

"That's rich, coming from you," I chided back.

And on it went as we drank and tried on clothing. I'd forgotten what carefree felt like. The emotion had always been so fleeting for me. A prisoner in my father's household had taught me to guard myself against everything, even moments like this. To not trust my friends, or the freedom I felt when I was with them.

I was a married woman now, but I didn't feel like Romeo's wife. More like his mistress, called on at his convenience. Or a hooker. A kept mistress could at least expect to be wooed and won from time to time. Most of what we did together was just sex.

More than a month had passed and I didn't know anything more about my enigmatic husband than the day I married him. I never made him breakfast, so I didn't know what his favorite food was. His favorite color? I hadn't a clue, but if I had to guess, I'd say black, as that was ninety percent of his wardrobe. Dark, like him and his moods. Our one unexpected date was the only time I'd seen him in a pair of jeans.

My increased security wasn't the only thing that changed after the dock explosion. I saw Romeo even less than usual. Often the only time I saw him at all was when he came home late and took me hard and fast before passing out. I would always wake up alone in the morning, which made me feel even more whorish. The only thing missing was money on my nightstand.

My sigh must have been loud because Neomi, who was standing closest to me, laced her fingers in mine and squeezed. "Are you okay, Vittoria?"

"Yes. Fine." I painted on my façade. "Thank you for asking."

I could tell she didn't believe me, but she didn't push for more information, thankfully, as I knew the unspoken rule in our world — *Silence is golden.*

Done shopping and a little tipsy, we paid for our purchases. Julius escorted me to the car. As I stepped in, I caught Leo typing on Gia's phone. Maybe he liked her after all. I pretended not to notice when he joined us a moment later.

"Where to, Mrs. Vitale?" he asked without making eye contact.

"It's Vittoria, Leo, please call me by my first name. Follow Gia, we're going to the beach."

Julius and Leo exchanged glances. "It's not safe," Julius rumbled. "Too public. We'll have to call for backup."

I slammed myself back into the seat to show my annoyance. "Fine, if you're calling the house anyway, have Esmeralda pack me a beach bag, and your *backup* can bring it with them and meet us there."

When we arrived, I chased everyone out of the car and had them face outward so I could change. This wasn't a well-planned day at all. We weren't even going to come to the beach until Gia suggested it as we walked outside into the gorgeous sunshine. Meh, why not be a little spontaneous once in a while? So what if my guards didn't like it? I used to escape all the time, they should be happy I hadn't pulled that on them yet.

Stepping out of the vehicle, I passed off my bag to Julius and strutted down the beach in a bikini that showed off everything. In fact, it was less a swimsuit than an artful arrangement of string. I was way more exposed than I'd been at the club, and I could see heads turning further down the beach. Some of them might even be taking photos. Knowing Romeo, I knew I ought to cover up, or even just leave, but that moment of common sense flew out the window on the wings of a little too much champagne.

I plunked myself down on the blankets beneath the umbrella Julius set up for me.

"Wow, V, you look stunning," Gia said admiringly, then smirked. "Are you sure your husband would approve?"

Good-natured teasing had always been part of our friendship, but for some reason, I bristled. "You know what, Gia? Mind your own business."

I left them all with their mouths agape and headed for the water. I walked out until the water was level with my chin and dove under.

I was a good swimmer, having grown up with a massive backyard pool. Drifting on my back with the waves gently bouncing me was just what I needed. I had just begun to relax when a hand popped out of the water beside me and clamped over my mouth.

"Shh, Vittoria, its Carlo," a familiar voice said. "Don't scream or you'll alert your guards."

I nodded and he removed his hand. He was on the open ocean side of my body so there was a good chance no one on shore could see his head bobbing just above the water line.

"I thought you were dead!" I blurted, then realized I wasn't far off. Most of his face was still healing from an obvious beat-down. Light green and yellowish bruises covered his chest and arms.

Carlo laughed bitterly. "It came close. Your husband did not appreciate the nature of your outing."

So it was my fault this had happened. "I'm sorry. Did you lose your job because of me?"

"It doesn't matter. I'm here for you, Vittoria."

I didn't like how that sounded and instinctively swam back a little. "What do you mean by, *for you?*"

He gave me one of his dazzling smiles. He really was a very good-looking man. "I couldn't leave you with that monster. You said you wanted to escape your husband. I came back to help you."

Panic bubbled inside of me, but why? This was the opportunity I'd been looking for all along, the one I'd given up on ever finding, so why wasn't I excited? I hadn't missed Carlo describing my husband as a monster. I hadn't found him so, despite his punishments and moods, but then, we were still in the honeymoon phase. Perhaps I should leave before he showed his true self.

I could go to South America, change my name and dye my hair and finally be free from the Calogeràs, the Vitales, the whole bloody business. Maybe, just maybe, I would find my prince charming there. I wasn't ready to give up on my childhood dream of finding the one who would make me a priority in his life before all else. For Romeo, *la familia* would always come first. He would look for me, yes, but he would eventually give up and remarry...

I was surprised at the flare of anger I felt when imagining my husband with another woman.

"What's the plan?" I asked.

"I hid a burner phone in your bag at the boutique. I'll send you the instructions. It will be random, Vittoria, as we have to move when your husband is occupied and so are your guards. It has to look like you left willingly. If we kill them, Romeo will think you have been kidnapped and won't stop searching for you, but if you just disappear, he'll assume you ran away like you've tried to before. He may not give chase, or even if he does, he knows your life isn't in danger so he will take his time and put out feelers, and by then, you'll be long gone."

"I understand and I'll make sure I'm ready when the time

comes." My heart was beating so hard in my chest with this scheme I was glad for the sounds of the water to hide it. "I better go, before they swim out here and get me. Thank you, Carlo, for not forgetting about me."

He disappeared beneath the waves, and I quickly swam to shore. The girls were downing vodka coolers and I joined them for one, but my mind was far away, deciding what was necessary to take and what could be left behind.

Gia nudged me meaningfully. "Have a nice swim?"

"Yes."

She leaned in close to me and whispered, "Don't worry. I'll pretend I didn't see that."

I blinked innocently and used my best confused voice. "I don't know what you mean."

"Oh please, girlfriend, save that for your husband. I saw Carlo out in the water."

I gripped Gia's arm and tugged her to her feet., cheerfully calling, "Gia and I are taking a little walk, be right back," as I dragged her away.

Once we were out of earshot, I released her arm. Gia just looked amused at my antics. She was a mafia brat herself, but so far down the line that she had little to no supervision in the family of eight children, especially with her being the youngest.

"Look, Gia, I know you don't take a lot of things seriously, but please, please take this situation as one of those things."

She lost the smirk immediately. "What's going on, V? Are you in danger?"

What could I say? If I gave away too much and she was questioned, I could see her cracking under the pressure. If I didn't say anything, she'd talk even faster. She might even ask questions of my own guards. I had to tell her something, and could only hope it wouldn't bite me in the ass down the road.

"For your own safety, I can't say much. But I'll tell you that Carlo was beaten and fired because of that night. If anyone finds out that he even talked to me again, they'll kill him, I'm sure."

Gia nodded solemnly. "But you won't tell me what you two were talking about?"

I sighed in resignation. It would be so nice to trust one of my best friends. I'd known Gia almost my entire life, but we didn't become friends until we were teenagers. At a family function, in which her entire family was in attendance, I became super bored and snuck away, losing my detail and in search of something more relevant to my thirteen-year-old self.

I found Gia hiding in the cloak room, looking at hot guys on a dating app. I dropped down beside her and we became fast friends. Out of my besties, she was the brattiest, and the least likely to conform to the traditions of our world.

I felt sorry for whoever she'd end up with one day. But, unlike myself, Gia would probably end up choosing her husband. There were five sisters and two brothers before her, and she'd been left alone for the most part. Many times, I'd been envious of her position in the family. Why couldn't my mother have given birth to enough babies to make me expendable? Then I wouldn't have had to marry Romeo in the first place.

And I wouldn't be contemplating leaving him. The pang in my stomach made me stop walking. If I did this, there was no going back, he'd never forgive me. But I wasn't given a choice and that was all I could see. My free will was taken from me, and I wouldn't ever stand for that.

Would I have chosen Romeo all on my own had I'd been given the choice?

The day of my wedding I would have said no darn way! But after all the intimate things we'd shared and how he made my body sing? I'd be a liar if I didn't hesitate to respond, perhaps.

"You, Elena, Neomi and Arianna will be the first ones they

question," I told Gia. "And you know Massimo. He won't relent until he gets the answers he wants."

Gia had the decency to shudder when I mentioned my brother-in-law. Romeo insisted he had a softer side, but Massimo had to be one of the most terrifying people to have to face. He was proportionately huge, and his eyes didn't go just dark like Romeo's when he was angry. No, they became menacing, and he almost always looked that way when he looked at me. The first time I'd seen it, I'd almost peed in fear. When I'd told Romeo later, he laughed and said that was his job.

"Is there anything I can do to help?"

Here comes the hard part. "I won't see you all for a while. Be patient and know that I am okay and will contact you when I can. Play stupid, Gia. You know nothing. Understand?"

She nodded. "Deal. But when you finally contact us, I'm first. After all, I've known you the longest."

"Deal," I said, glad to have dodged the bullet. "Are you sure no one else saw Carlo?"

She looked back at our friends, now teasing my guards as they waited for us to return. "Are you kidding? Those two are practicing their seduction skills. And the men are trying not to notice. Kind of funny, don't you think?"

"Well, if you're asking, I think watching Neomi try to get Leo to notice her is hilarious. Speaking of Leo, I saw you with him when we left the store. What was that about?"

Gia winked. "I have myself a date with the big lug. There is something dark and sinister about him, and oh, so sexy!"

Leo was wearing dark sunglasses so I couldn't see his eyes, but I could feel him from here and Gia was right, he emanated a dangerous vibe that was hard to ignore. Even with the glasses on, I knew he was looking right at us and suddenly I felt a chill.

"He's definitely intense," I said with a shudder. "Come on, let's join the others. I have to leave soon and I want to spend a bit more time with you all, before... you know."

Gia laughed. "I don't, actually, but yeah, let's join them. Neomi is standing way too close to Leo."

An hour later, we packed up and left the beach. I said goodbye to my friends and got in the car and as soon as I did, my phone lit up with a message from my husband.

"I see my marks have faded, wife. It's time for a reminder of who you belong to."

A shiver moved through me and not entirely of fear. Why did I love hearing those words so much?

Leo was on one side of me and Julius on the other. In the front was another guard and the driver. Four huge men and I was sandwiched between them. Thank goodness they were loyal to my husband, because in any other situation, this would be scary.

Donatello, the driver, cracked the window and as the warm air circulated around the car, I caught a quick whiff of that familiar scent, the one that I couldn't quite place. Studying each of the men, nothing came to me. I regulated the smell to unsolved in my brain. Probably an aftershave that someone I know wore and it didn't matter whom.

When the car pulled into the driveway, I could see a light on in my bedroom window. My husband was waiting. I went as slowly as I dared, knowing it was time to pay the piper, except I didn't want to pay. Or did I?

CHAPTER THIRTEEN

Romeo

We were on my private jet, flying to Italy for the annual meeting, but my thoughts weren't on the danger I was walking into every time I came to one of these events or the details that would keep me safe while I was here. Instead, my time with Vittoria last night consumed me.

It was one thing to see the images on my phone of her in the skimpy bikini. But seeing her strut into our room like a bronzed goddess had my cock standing at attention.

Massimo had chosen well when he'd picked Leo. Unlike Carlo, he kept me informed of where my wife was at all times and what she was wearing. The fact a dozen of my men witnessed her wearing almost nothing angered me, and that any number of total strangers could enjoy what belonged to me pissed me off like nothing before.

White hot rage consumed me when I received the photo. When he told me that my wife's personal maid had sent it, I felt slightly more forgiving toward Vittoria. She'd only worn the swimsuit she'd been given, although she still should have wrapped up with a towel. But the maid who picked that suit out of the many in her closet? I fired her on the spot.

My mother talked me out of it and although I relented and allowed her to stay, it was as my mother's attendant. From now on, I would oversee everything to do with my wife and anyone who didn't obey my rules would be lucky to only be fired!

Vittoria's eyes radiated challenge when she stopped about two feet in front of where I sat on the end of the bed and cocked a hip. She was such a saucy brat!

"Perhaps you should at least appear repentant, Vittoria. Daddy is very displeased with you." I watched in pleasure as her pupils dilated, and the pulse at her throat quickened. "Did you feel ignored, *Principessa*? I best remedy that."

Reaching out, I tugged her between my legs, boxing her in, and undid the string that barely held the two triangles of material together, uncovering her nipples. Bringing her arms to the front of her body, I wrapped the material around her wrists, binding them. Her upper arms pressed her breasts together, making a lovely feast.

Keeping her locked in place with my thighs, I reached up and snagged a nipple, torturing it to a point. Vittoria dropped her head, eyes slit as she immersed herself in the sensation I delivered.

I repeated this action on the other breast, her breathy pants coming out faster and louder the more I pinched and rolled the sensitive bud. Releasing her, I stood up and tugged her arms over her head, attaching the bikini strings to a clamp that kept her arms fully extended above her head where she stood.

Fucking gorgeous! Her nipples were so hard they could cut glass. She was already in subspace. She went there fast these days, as she was very responsive to my dominance over her body.

She watched as I unsheathed my belt from my pants and

folded it in half, snapping it in the air. She jumped the first time, but after her initial shock, she licked her lips and watched me, waiting for me to deliver the pain and pleasure she craved.

Keeping the stroke light, I flicked her nipple with the belt. Her eyes widened in surprise but didn't protest. I flicked the other nipple, a little harder, gauging her response. Her head dropped back, a low moan escaping her throat.

I took a nipple in my mouth and clamped down on the soft flesh.

"Oh! Yes!" she hissed.

"You were a naughty girl, Vittoria. Why should Daddy reward you?"

Her head snapped up. "But it wasn't my fault, Daddy! That's what Esmeralda sent me."

I spanked the tip of her wet nipple with the belt.

"Aaugh!"

"You could have covered up, wife. You know how much it bothers me when you allow other men to ogle your body. Did you want me to gouge out some eyeballs? That's what you want, for me to blind an entire generation of men?"

"No! I'm sorry. Please don't hurt anyone. You're right I was naughty, and I wanted to get your attention so even though I didn't choose the swimsuit, I could have covered up, but I didn't."

I took her other nipple in my mouth and clamped down. Vittoria cried out as a powerful orgasm rocked her body. Her climax wept down her legs to her sandaled feet. She was a goddess and all *mine*!

"I don't know if you're sorry. Maybe I will have to take out some eyes, beginning with your security team."

"No, Romeo! Please don't punish them, punish me instead."

This was a new game between us. I put the blame for her actions at others' feet and she begged to be the recipient of their punishment. Then I gave her exactly what she craved until every ounce of resistance was gone from her body.

I turned her body to face the bed and ripped her bikini bottoms in two. She was naturally tanned, but her time in the sun had made her skin darker, a stark contrast to the paleness of her trembling globes.

"Widen your legs and don't move."

My belt made a whizzing sound as it cut through the air before landing on her backside. Vittoria rose onto the balls of her feet with a slight swing forward of her hips. I watched the belt mark bloom on her perfect ass, relishing the sight. She was such a brat — a gorgeous, perfect brat.

The belt sung as it whipped through the air before landing on top of the previous stripe.

She cried out but jutted her ass out as far as she could. My wife really was a dichotomy and I loved both parts in equal measure.

I landed a dozen stripes before she tried to escape the punishment by dancing on her toes and twisting in place. I didn't want to hurt the sensitive flesh of her hips, but I wasn't about to stop so soon.

I released her arms and sat down on a bench in our room, tugging her over my lap. "You've been a very naughty girl, Vittoria. Beg Daddy for forgiveness."

A fresh release of excitement made her swollen lips shiny. She loved it when I spoke dirty to her.

"I'm so sorry, Daddy. Will you forgive me?"

She played the role of a little girl so well, I wondered sometimes if that was a true aspect of her personality. But as it never showed beyond these sessions, I assumed that she really enjoyed getting into her role as Daddy's brat.

"I will. But not yet." I parted her thighs so each one hung over my large thigh. I brought my hand down with some force over the raised pink stripes and she yelped and tried to move, but in this position, she was locked in place.

I continued to bring my hand down, landing stinging swats on her sensitive sit spot until it was bright fire engine red. The tears of remorse started and so did the begging, but I wasn't done yet.

Down her thighs, I went – *splat, thwack, thud, crack* – until my naughty girl hung limply over my thighs. The length of time it took to arrive at the place of acceptance was much longer than usual, causing me to question, why? Had something happened while she was out that I hadn't heard about?

I ran one hand over her hot skin and down the slickness between her thighs. Vittoria moaned, widening her legs, encouraging me to give her the relief she so desired, but I withheld it.

"Do you have something to say to me, Vittoria?" I asked warningly.

"I'm sorry for being naughty. Will you please finish the punishment, *Daddy?*"

Was it wrong that when she called me that I grew harder than a rock? Running my fingers through her dampness, I lubricated them and sunk two into her tight rear entrance.

"Fuck me, Daddy!"

Lord, have mercy on me! This wife of mine scorched every part of me, driving my need for her until I didn't think I could take anymore.

Scooping her into my arms, I stood and placed her over the end of the bed. Grabbing lube from my drawer, I shucked my pants in record time and got my hard shaft slick, pumping it in my hand.

"Open for me, *Principessa*."

Vittoria reached back and spread her cheeks with her hands and then gazed at me over her shoulder, her expression pleading, reflecting my desperation to be inside of her. I held her gaze while I pressed my cock past the tight ring of muscle and slammed home as deep as I could.

Her eyes almost rolled back in her head with the invasion.

"Are you Daddy's little slut?" I fucked her hard as a variety of mewls and moans poured from her parted lips.

"Yes. Yes! Fuck me, Daddy. Fuck your little slut!"

I smacked her hands out of the way and grasped her hips. I drove inside of her, pulling out to the tip and drilling back inside. Two more strokes and Vittoria was screaming her release to the world, except our room was soundproof, so only I heard the primal pleasure that was her orgasm.

Her muscles squeezed so tight I thought my cock would break off. But I kept at it until I felt a zing down my spine to my balls and I erupted like a volcano, filling her tight ass with my lava.

Vittoria collapsed while I gently pulled free from her. A sigh of contentment like a cat with a full belly of cream followed from her swollen lips. She curled into a ball on the bed reminding me even more of a satisfied cat.

Later, we showered and made slow love while I pulled promises of obedience from her. Long after she fell asleep, I lay awake. Something wasn't right, but for the life of me, I couldn't put my finger on what.

I went over the itinerary and rechecked that the estate was well guarded even though I had two dozen soldiers with me, the best of my crew. The unspoken rule in our household was if Massimo and I were gone overnight, one of the other brothers needed to be in residence. They all had suites at the house for this very reason.

This time, it was Tony at home. My brother was brilliant when it came to numbers because he was a control freak, and his dark side ran even deeper than mine which garnered him the nickname *The Beast*. He was a deadly shot and known for never leaving anyone alive. I had left him in charge of the

soldiers guarding the estate for the next few days and specifi-
cally to watch Vittoria.

"Everything is fine, Romeo, relax."

Simo sat opposite me, as always, dissecting me based on my
expression. I knew I must have looked pensive, and he didn't
miss it.

"I know, but my gut is telling me something isn't right."

"Our men in Siderna are in place already. Our snipers are set
up and if anyone pulls anything, we'll drop them before anyone
knows what's going on."

I sighed, suddenly feeling a lot older than my thirty-seven
years. "It's not me I'm worried about, it's Vittoria."

He cracked a smile. "You know I wasn't sure about her for
the longest time. She's a complete brat. Mouthy and too smart
for her own good. But more recently, I've seen how loyal she is
to you and how much she loves you."

Love? She'd never uttered those three little words again — *I
love you*. So how did Massimo know? Was it that obvious to
everyone... except me?

"She's a good actress," I said. "Don't be fooled."

His grim mien lightened when his lips curled into a shallow
smile. "I see it when she looks at you. The love in her eyes is
very evident, Romeo. So, let's toss away those seeds of doubt.
Vittoria is fine, we are fine, and we'll be home in a few days."

He was right. I was acting paranoid.

My phone dinged, a text alert from Vinny. He was clearly
holding his phone and taking a selfie with my wife. On her
other side was a very serious-looking Tony, trying to smile while
glaring at Vinny's arm around my wife. I trusted Vinny
completely, but they looked good together. Only six years apart
they looked more like a couple than she and I did, and it pissed
me off.

"Take your arm off my wife." I texted back.

His response was to send another picture. This time, he had

my wife tucked into his side and they were both winking. Why, that little brat! I'd get her back for that.

Now a text from Vittoria: "Sorry, he made me."

"Do you think that little excuse will save you from the big bad daddy wolf?" I sent back to her and then waited a full minute before she sent — "I hope not." With a heart emoji.

"Good girl. Behave yourself and you have my full permission to tell Vincenzo to go fuck himself."

She sent back a laughy face. Chuckling, I tossed my phone down on the table and found Massimo studying me intently. The smile left my face, the façade sliding back into place.

"I never thought I'd see the day," Simo remarked.

"What day?" I asked in a dark, serious tone.

"The one where the great Romeo actually fell in love."

Hmph. "You've said that before, but I think your eyes deceive you, brother." If my feelings were that obvious, I was in serious trouble. It was one thing for my brothers to know my weaknesses, but our world was full of enemies. Vittoria just became the largest liability in my life.

CHAPTER FOURTEEN

Vittoria

My punishment had been incredible, and I lay like a boneless fish in my bed, reliving all the delicious things my husband had done to me. I was thinking about getting up and showering when my burner phone rang.

Quickly reaching into my nightstand, I pulled it out. "Carlo?" I answered.

"It is. Listen up. Today is the day. I heard through the grapevine that Romeo and Massimo are in the air, and they took a large contingent of their men with them. Antonio has been tasked with staying at the estate and keeping an eye on things. Apparently, your husband doesn't trust you to not get into trouble. We need to act after he's arrived and checked in with the security at home. It will be the first thing he does, and then he will let his guard down a bit. That is when you will make your quiet exit."

Before I could ask any questions. The phone went dead. I

guess he would be calling me back with exactly how I would be making a *quiet exit*.

Moving from the bed, the plushness of the area rug grabbed my attention and my focus on my surroundings became hyper-aware. The birds outside, the way the sunlight slanted into the bedroom, and on our bed.

How many steps to the Italian marbled ensuite? The smells of citrus, and bergamot — Romeo, and the scents of my body care intertwined — mango and vanilla... assaulted more than my nostrils, but also tugged my heart.

In the past few months, against all reasoning, Romeo and I had become a couple. Maybe not like normal couples, but wasn't that overrated anyway?

In the shower, an internal argument raged inside of me: do I, don't I? What do I really want? Every insecurity I'd ever faced paraded around in my head, making things worse. My inner little princess was shaking her head at me, but what did she know anyway? My tiny toddler brain created her, and my childhood sustained and grew the fantasy of the perfect man.

The woman I'd become wasn't as committed to a man as she was to her freedom. I wanted to escape the tower, even if it was safe, and lead a life of independence. Then why were my guts twisting into knots at the idea of leaving here, leaving *him*?

Out of the shower, I grabbed my phone and called Gia.

"Hot stuff here, how can I direct your call?" she answered.

I burst out laughing. "And everyone thinks I'm a brat. You're so much worse!"

"You are a brat, Vittoria, a sneaky one. I'm more of an in-your-face kinda brat."

I rolled my eyes, even though she couldn't see me.

"So why did you call?"

"I need your help," I answered in a quiet voice. The danger of my situation settled in the pit of my stomach like a lead weight.

"Is this about our talk at the beach?" Her voice had lost the bratty sarcastic tone.

"Yeah. I need to ask you a question. If someone offered you freedom, would you take it? What I mean to say, if you could choose between what your family wanted you to do and what you always wanted to do, what would you pick?"

I held the phone like a lifeline waiting for Gia to give me her answer, and when she did, I was a little surprised.

"Vittoria. No matter what, life is a choice. You can stay, you can go, you can dress as a drag queen or become a cliff diver. Whatever you choose, remember that you are choosing it, so do it wisely."

Well, what do I do with that? "Not what I was looking for, but thanks just the same."

"Wait, Victoria. Whatever you decide, I'll be here."

That helped a little. To know that whatever happened, Gia at least would be on my team.

"Thanks. I gotta go. Later." I hung up and lay back on the bed looking to the ceiling for answers that weren't coming. A knock on the door sometime later brought me back to the present.

"Vittoria?" One of Romeo's brothers, but I wasn't sure which one by his voice alone.

"Yes?"

"It's Vinny. I'm making lunch if you would like to come and join us."

What was he doing here in the middle of the day? "Uh, sure. I need about half an hour, I just got out of the shower."

"Okay. See you in the kitchen when you're ready."

Half an hour later, the sound of laughter reached me as I traversed the long walkway to the kitchen. Vinny, Tony, and their mother, Isabella, stood around the island while Vinny busied himself making lunch.

The afternoon light streamed through the huge bank of

windows, framing the domestic scene in a halo of sunshine. All three looked up when I entered.

"There she is." Isabella came and kissed me on each cheek like she always did. The woman was so warm and friendly. Then she held me at arms' length. "Are you well, daughter?"

I buried my angst and turned on the charm. "Never better, but I'm starving and heard we have a 5-star chef today."

Vinny dropped the wooden spoon he'd been stirring a sauce with and pulled me into a hug. Tony growled at him, sounding exactly like a beast, but Vinny just laughed.

"Don't be so grumpy, Antonio." He quickly took a selfie with me and Tony who looked less than impressed. Isabella chuckled and shook her head muttering something about boys being boys and took up stirring the sauce on the stove.

Vinny laughed about something. Then grabbed me and told me to wink and snapped another picture. "Rom's not happy," he chuckled.

"Are you trying to get me into trouble? You know I do that well enough on my own."

Vinny laughed harder but Tony only offered a slight nod. I tugged my phone out of my pocket and texted my husband.

"Sorry, he made me."

I didn't expect a reply, but my phone beeped and I opened it to see this. "Do you think that little excuse will save you from the big bad daddy wolf?"

Holy hell! Desire zipped through me and settled deep inside my core. I started to answer eagerly only to remember I was leaving him. For a long moment, I could not think or feel anything but pain, but I couldn't just leave it at that.

"I hope not." I answered lamely and added a red heart.

His response made me laugh.

"Good girl. Behave yourself and you have my full permission to tell Vincenzo to go fuck himself."

"Was that Rom? What did he say?" Vinny asked from his position back at the stove.

"I can't repeat it in polite company but basically, to screw off!"

A gruff chuckle from Tony and a beaming smile from Vinny.

After a delicious lunch, Tony excused himself, kissing Isabella and telling Vinny to behave himself. I left too, saying I had some things to do, and beelined back to my room to listen for my burner phone to ring.

Not five minutes later, it went off. Taking a deep breath, I answered the call.

"I've changed my mind. I'm staying."

"What?" he said sharply, then blew a hard breath into the phone and lowered his voice. "Don't make up your mind until you have all the information. There are things you don't know, Vittoria, things I've learned about Romeo. You may change your mind once you know what kind of man he really is."

That was unexpected. "What kind of things?"

He responded with images of Romeo getting blowjobs and lap dances, photo after photo, so many different women. I scrolled over them in rapid succession, dizzy and sick to my stomach. Surely these couldn't be current, but I looked at the time stamps and they were all taken since we'd been married. Son of a bitch!

This changed everything. "What do I need to do?"

CHAPTER FIFTEEN

Romeo

Six hours of discussing shipping and transportation later, I was ready for a break. A message came through from Fausto during the long meeting regarding the identity of the ghost who went by the name of Ardo and who had been a thorn in my side, since.

More accurately, he had been a thorn in my ass since the agreement with Santo Calogerà, who was noticeably absent from the meeting today. Despite the so-called peace that had existed between us since the union of our families, I didn't trust that man and agreed with my brother that he was up to something.

The moment we were outdoors, we returned Fausto's call.

"Hey. What do you have?"

"I followed through with Tony and followed the numbers, which led me to tapping into the security feed and found some that had been erased. It's not great but I do have a partial image of the one they call the Ghost."

An image appeared on my phone.

"It can't be," I heard myself say. "What the hell?"

"What?" Massimo peered over my shoulder. It was only partial but there was no mistaking the face. It was Leo.

"But you vetted him," I said, not accusingly but just stunned.

"Carlo vetted him," Massimo said and pulled out his phone. "Fausto. Check on the family. We've got a lead on our mole problem and it's Vittoria's new head of security. Find the old one, too. He knows our estate and must have others working with him."

"On it."

He hung up and I texted my wife.

Nothing came back. *Dio Santo!*

Massimo was talking a mile a minute in Italian to whomever was on the other end. I phoned Tony and was about to hang up after a dozen rings when my brother picked up, and before either of us could say anything, the sounds of screams and gunfire came through the line.

"Tony, where's Vittoria?" I demanded. "Tony! What the fuck is going on?"

"We were attacked," he said groggily. "Inside job. I was knocked out and I'm just coming to. I don't know anything, brother. I'll call you back when we lock this shit down!"

Massimo was still firing rapid orders in Italian. *Cazzo!* I was done waiting for status or damage reports and called my pilot. "Get things ready. I want to leave in half an hour," I ordered, and hung up at the same time as Massimo. "Well?"

"Leo and Ardo are the same guy. Leonardo –get ready for this – Calogerà."

A string of curse words poured from me. "How is it possible that we didn't know about his existence? Who is he, a cousin? Nephew?"

"I don't know yet, but Simon finally got a hit on this guy and that's how we got his name. He's still digging."

"Speaking of Simon, how did our estate get infiltrated without him being alerted? Or was he in on it? Whoever the hell Leonardo Calogerà is, he obviously had help."

He was about to answer when a call came through from Tony. "Get everyone to the plane, we're leaving," I told Simo, and to Tony, barked, "Speak to me."

"At least five of our men were in on it," he said without preamble.

"Simon?" I guessed.

"No, but he's alive," Tony told me. "Said Julius came to see him, something about clearing Vittoria to leave the grounds, said he cleared it with you already. Simon tried to call and confirm and got his skull cracked, but he's sitting up now and talking. Tano's looking him over now."

"Take care of him," I said, feeling a twinge of remorse at how quickly I'd suspected him. And Julius, a mole! I'd known the man my whole life, one of my father's closest confidants. I would have trusted him with my life, and had, many times. "What else?"

"We managed to take one of them alive. We'll keep him on ice until you get here."

"Vittoria?" I asked, but somehow, I knew. If she'd been safe, he would have led with that.

"She's gone, brother. They took her and not just her, Romeo. They managed to get a hold of Vinny as well. We've got feed of them both being thrown in a van."

I calculated the time it would take to fly back and was about to issue orders. They knew I would be away, they knew how long it would take to fly back, and most importantly, they knew I *would* come back for this. They weren't in any rush, just dangling the carrot to make me act carelessly.

"Tony, we need as much information as possible before we act. Have Simon turn on all the trackers for Vittoria." There was one they would never find, but he didn't need to know that right now. "Then have him find all Calogerà businesses in the area, even the shell companies. While he is working on that, pull all your men that you trust from wherever they are stationed and bring them to the estate. We need a thorough check for bugs and devices. They could be listening to our plans, right now. Start the search in Simon's office and when it's safe, have him call me directly."

"Got it, boss, anything else?"

"Yes. Be careful, proceed with caution, and keep your communications written until the house has been thoroughly searched and every last man accounted for. Oh, and one more thing. Find Vittoria's call log and see who the last person she talked to was, and bring them to the house."

"Okay, boss, on it." Tony hung up and like magic, Massimo was there with the car. Our driver made record time to the airstrip while I was on the phone. I typed a message into my phone and showed it to Massimo.

He nodded and silently had the men search for listening devices. Before the plane left the ground, we found them all, seven in total. *Porca puttana!*

"This has been in the works for a while, Romeo," Massimo commented.

"A good long while. Our defenses were never intended to guard against an inside threat. We will need to take another look at how we do things in the future. For now, we play their game. They timed this, they'll know when we land and that's when they'll make contact. They probably also know we took a captive, who most likely knows nothing, like the last ones we took. I bet those fuckers are congratulating themselves right now on pulling one over on us."

We sat in silence until a call came from Simon.

"What did you find?"

"Leonardo is the son of Don Santo Calogerà, he's Vittoria's brother."

"*Cazzo!*" Could things get any worse?

"There's more, boss. We haven't been able to confirm if Vittoria knew about the attack."

And there it was, things getting worse. I thought back to the past several weeks with my wife, looking for signs that she was a betrayer and working for my enemy. She was smart and tenacious, but could she be part of something of this magnitude?

Possibly. She always fought against being bartered into marriage. Maybe my mistake was in believing that she'd been raised to be a mafia queen and had accepted her fate. Still, had she been so disgruntled, would her body have responded to me as it did? Would she have told me she loved me? I replayed that moment when I saw something hidden behind her wall, a girl with a secret.

"She is my wife," I reminded him. "She will be treated as a victim until we get her back and find out for ourselves."

Massimo didn't respond, which was fine with me. I needed to think and strategize the best way to get my wife and brother back, preferably unscathed. What I had been holding back on was what they may be doing to them right now. If Vittoria was in on the scheme, which I didn't believe, yet, then she would no doubt be celebrating the temporary win.

If she didn't know about her brother, what type of fucked up mind games would he be playing with her? My knuckles turned white as I gripped the arm rests. I would destroy anyone who hurt her. No matter what, Vittoria was mine and she knew I would come for her.

I was sure that Vinny had allowed himself to be captured on purpose. He would run interference and keep the attention on himself for as long as he could. No one could be as sneaky as our youngest brother. Even when he was two years old, the toddler could hide from us all day long. He was smart, wily, and a good actor, and could play both sides.

Massimo's phone dinged with a message alert.

"It's from Simon. The last person Vittoria spoke with was her girlfriend, Gia. How would you like to handle her interrogation?"

"I'll let you handle her. I'm in no mood for games and may kill her if she gets mouthy on me."

Despite the levity of the situation, Massimo chuckled. "She truly is a brat, but I understand this woman and will extract what I need to from her, my way.

The timing wasn't appropriate, but I couldn't help sparing a moment to consider the slightly adoring look in his eyes when Simo spoke of Gia. Did he like her? *Mama Mia!*

* * *

We pulled through the gate of my property, which now resembled the set of a war movie, given all the soldiers strategically placed around us. Tony came down the steps to open my door the instant we came to a stop, and hustled me into the house under cover of six men with Massimo following behind us.

"Is Gia here?" Massimo asked.

Tony didn't spare a glance back at his brother. 'Yeah, in your office, as requested."

Massimo took a different passage and would hopefully learn the nature of Gia and Vittoria's conversation. I followed Tony on to the war room.

At the table was Massimo's number one, Dante, Simon, our head of security and resident IT expert, Fausto, Gaetano, Giovani, and myself. Beyond the soundproof room was the holding area where our captive enemy was trussed up like a Thanksgiving sacrifice awaiting the death stroke.

"Tony, you've been on the ground here. Bring us up to speed."

"I thought we'd start with the footage that Simon was able to recover." Tony nodded at Simon, who brought up the feed. The massive screen at the head of our table showed Carlo stalking down the hallway towards my suite. From another hallway came Leo.

With no cameras in my suite, the image held on Leo in the hallway, while Carlo brought out a series of pictures. My cameras were of the highest quality and I could make out enough to recognize blown-up photos of me at Club Savage, with a variety of different women. They were real enough, but taken well before my marriage, some of them years ago, but Vittoria wouldn't know that.

A tear slid down Vittoria's cheek, but she handed them back and shook her head. Leo said something more, trying to convince her, but she turned around to go back inside, and when she did, Carlo swiftly placed a cloth over her nose and mouth. She fought, but she was no match for him and he held her until she passed out.

"Chloroform. *Sporco bastardo!*" Tano spit out.

"Dirty bastards, indeed. But it does prove that Vittoria had nothing to do with this. Even if she thought I had betrayed her, she wouldn't go with them."

"There's more, Romeo."

From the same hallway Carlo took, now came eight men in vests and masks. Leo said something and they moved off in groups of four down each wing.

The camera angle switched and we were seeing them moved into groups of two, knocking out Tony, and several of our staff before anyone knew what was going down. Vinny, who was in the kitchen with our mother stepped in front of her. He put up a good fight, but when two more soldiers rushed in, Vinny held up his hands in surrender. The cameras had no sound, but we could see his mouth moving: *Take me*. Apparently, the soldiers couldn't resist a willing victim, so they bound and blindfolded him, but they oddly balked at taking my mother prisoner as well. Instead, they almost seemed to show her a kind of curt respect, seating her in a chair and tying her to it. One of them even straightened her skirt to cover her legs before they moved out the front of the house, shooting a few soldiers that weren't knocked out, along the way.

Their job completed, the soldiers regrouped in the driveway, entered two separate nondescript blacked-out vehicles and drove away.

"Have we learned the location of their whereabouts?"

"Well, I looked at Julius and Leo's driving history first, but you got to understand, they knew our vehicles were in the system, so there's nothing there but what they logged. And they brought their own vehicles for the big job, obviously. That leaves only the tracker apps on their phones. No," he said, as I began a frustrated response. "Not Julius and Leo's. Obviously, they'd have ditched theirs. But Vinny's still got his. I don't know where he put it that they missed it when they were tying him up, but he had it and it's still on. And they may have left Vittoria's phone behind, but she's still got the chip in her wedding ring. Here."

Simon brought up a map on the big screen with a few flashing red lights on the overlay in the general shape of an inverted V. "Here's Vinny's ping-trail, with time-stamps. Looks like they got out of the city, drove another half-hour and stopped somewhere around here." He sketched an unnecessary circle around the top dot. "That's the cell tower, of course, not the cell phone, but the phone had to be close. Signal doesn't move for a good twenty minutes, then it goes this way and eventually ends up at the east docks.

"You're assuming Vinny's still with it and they haven't just chucked it in the ocean," I said, outwardly calm while inside, I couldn't help wondering if my brother's corpse was at the bottom of the ocean with it.

"I'm not assuming anything. But it's a lead and I'm looking into it. Now here's Vittoria's trail."

The red dots vanished and a series of blue ones came on, and even before Simon brought Vinny's trail back, I could see hers ended where his had stalled before moving off east. "What's out there?" I asked. "Airport?"

"No. That's the first thing I checked for." Simon brought up a satellite image of the area, mostly open fields with a few structures and highways chopping up the landscape. I'm looking into who owns what as we speak and if any of it has changed hands recently —"

"Or not so recently," I interrupted. "This wasn't an impulse. They had moles in our house, they had gunmen and drivers, they had their own vehicles, they had a very limited window of attack. That means they had a staging point. Someplace relatively close, but isolated." I tapped one of the boxy buildings on-screen, then another and another. "Find out who owns these. Calogerà is behind this. Start with his subsidiaries and shell companies."

"Already on it," Simon promised, typing away.

Massimo entered the war room.

I turned to him at once. "Did you find out anything?"

He nodded. "Carlo showed up to the beach day with the girls. He swam out from the point so no one on land saw him, except Gia, and Vittoria, of course. Gia says it didn't look like Vittoria was expecting him, but they talked for a few minutes and then he swam away. All Vittoria would tell her was that Carlo was there to help her. And then later, told her it was for her own safety as she knew we would question her friend group."

The pieces all fell into place. No wonder Carlo had allowed Vittoria to go to the club, dress how she wanted, do what she wanted... and make sure I was there to find out, knowing I'd punish her for it. He'd been gaining her trust, making me the villain, even to the point of taking a swing at Massimo when he'd been fired, knowing he'd be badly beaten but left alive out of respect for all his years of service. He'd want to be wearing bruises when he offered my wife a lifeline to freedom.

Vittoria, in the hands of the enemy... Every moment that I stood here, she was in their grip. I wanted to believe that Calogerà wouldn't harm his own daughter, but I wouldn't bet her life on it.

Leaving Simon to do his cyber-thing, I entered the cold room to get information the old-fashioned way.

I could see our prisoner had been shot, and my guys had worked him over some, but they'd been careful not to do any permeant damage and his bullet wounds had been treated by Gaetano, and only because I wished him alive, for now.

Cazzo! It was Donatello, Vittoria's driver. Was anyone loyal? I nodded at the two soldiers standing guard to leave us.

"How do you wish to die, Donatello?"

He was pale beneath the mottled bruising on his face, but defiant.

"Whatever. I'm dying anyway."

"Yes, you will, but let me be more specific." I bent over him and despite his bravado, he shrank back, even paler. "Do you want to die a whole man? Do you want us to bring your body to your pregnant girlfriend tonight and let her bury you with honor, believing you fell protecting the family? Hm?" I opened my mouth in a feral grin. "Or should we bring her here, and make her share your execution? When we take an arm off you, we take an arm off her. We take a leg off you, we take a leg off her. We slice open your belly —"

His desperate face broke. "You wouldn't kill an innocent!"

He was right, but I wouldn't let him know that.

"The sins of the father are carried by the sons," I reminded him. "Are you going to die a sinner, Donatello? Or are you going to confess and let your woman bury you with honor?"

He moaned and thrashed in his chair, cursing me.

"So you want her to die," I said mildly. "All right, but don't say I didn't give you a choice. I did and you chose to kill her, and your unborn baby, and for what, your loyalty to those traitorous fucks?!"

He dropped his head, defeated. "They left me behind, so I guess I owe them nothing, and I'm sure you've figured it out by now anyway."

"Santo Calogerà," I said. "And his son."

Donatello spat blood and laughed bitterly. "This plan has been in the works for several years. Santo always meant to offer you the docks, then raid the shipments until your allies broke faith with you. Once you became a liability to the council, he could kill you and your brothers without retaliation, and the new Don would give him back his docks to broker a new peace."

"Don Carlo, I presume. Tell me, what have I done to make him, and you, betray me like this?"

"You're weak," Donatello spat. "Your father was a great man, but I'll be damned if I stand by and let his empire fall into the hands of a bunch of queers and fry-cooks! And the pussy-whipped *boy* who tolerates them!"

"And Vittoria? How does she fit in the plan?"

"A pawn only. He couldn't just give you the docks and you wouldn't make an offer for them, so he had to get them to you somehow. As a wedding present, ha. I imagine she knows the truth now, eh, *cazzone*! I can just see that snotty bitch —"

Before he could utter another word, I punched him in the mouth.

"Be careful, *testa di cazzo*, that's my wife you are talking about, and no one disrespects Vittoria. Where are they hiding her?"

Donatello kept his head dropped, silent.

I whipped out my phone and showed him a picture of his pregnant wife, and the car parked outside of his brownstone. "Talk!"

"How the hell should I know? Do I look like I'm with them?"

I punched him again. "You knew the plan. Now talk!"

"For what it's worth, the boss is waiting at an abandoned slaughterhouse at the edge of town. As for your brother..." The fucker had the audacity to smirk at me. "Taking him wasn't in the plan. I have no idea where he is."

"I do. They took him to the east docks." I punched him again. "Any idea why?"

He spit blood on the floor, then glared up at me. "I don't know."

"Not good enough." I punched him again. "What's waiting for me at the east docks, *cazzo*?"

"I don't fucking know! It wasn't part of the fucking plan!"

"Then why the east docks?"

"Because they hate you and want to humiliate you! I'm telling you, I don't know. All I can guess is, killing your brother at your place of business, where you obviously no longer have control would be like the final nail in the coffin for your family."

Shit. I needed to shift gears. We needed three teams and I knew that mine would be the smallest, it had to be a surprise attack.

"Last question before you meet your maker. How do I get into the slaughterhouse where they are keeping my wife undetected? Don't lie to me. Your woman will be riding in the car with me."

He licked his bloody lips. "Don't take the main road in, they'll be watching. A mile or so further down is a dirt pathway, just wide enough for a vehicle. It will take you behind the building and then you can sneak in through the side door."

I pulled my gun from my waistband. I was going to leave him for one of the soldiers to finish off, but I wanted to watch the light go out of his eyes. As I've said, I can be a prick. But he'd sealed his fate when he helped those who took my wife and brother.

I pressed the gun against his forehead.

He was ready to die, but a flicker of fear touched his eyes, not for his own life, but for another's. "And my —"

I fired the gun and sent him to Hell with doubt in his heart

I heard scrambling outside and the door flew open. "Boss?"

"Clean up this mess, would you? And send his ring to his woman so she knows he's not coming back." I paused, then added in a rough voice, "Tell her he died protecting his family."

"Yes, sir."

I wiped my hands off and returned to the war room. "Simon, stop what you're doing and start looking for an old slaughterhouse."

"Old..." Brow furrowed, Simon did his thing and slowly nodded. "Yeah, looks like a lot of these fields are part of an old cattle range owned by the Cooper Ranch, and... yeah, about ten years ago, this bit here was auctioned off."

I studied the map where he indicated, but of course, all it showed me was a bird's eye view of an L-shaped building in the middle of overgrown nowhere. "The slaughterhouse?"

"It used to be the Cooper cattle processing plant, but it hasn't been in operation for thirty, forty years. Like I say, they auctioned it and some surrounding acreage off ten years ago to a company called..." More typing. "NARDO Development," Simon said triumphantly.

Massimo and I exchanged glances. "Leo," I said grimly.

"He sure does like the sound of his own name," Massimo agreed.

"Massimo, we need a triple attack. You will take your best short-range shooters with you to the Cooper place. Be loud enough to get the attention of anyone watching, but don't be too obvious. I want someone in the trees, behind cars, *capiche?*"

"Yes, boss."

"Tano, we are the same build and have very similar looks. You go with Simo, wearing my clothing, and be me at that location. Act like a crazy husband when you break through the front door, but keep your face covered. We need to make this look legit and if Massimo is there, they will expect me to be as well. I'll take Tony, Fausto, and the best of the long-range shooters with me. Everyone else goes to the docks to bring Vinny back. We only have one chance to take them by surprise."

"You realize this is all about you," Tano said. Others may find him dark and aloof, and he was with most people. He was a strategist both on the operating table and for our family. "They're trying to lure you out and you're letting them."

Murmurs of assent from the rest seated around the table.

"Those fuckers broke into my house and took my family. I will not be staying home. I will be the man making holes in the chests of men who betrayed me." I stood, propelled to my feet by the anger thrumming through me. "Not even God will keep those fuckers safe from me!"

CHAPTER SIXTEEN

Vittoria

Moaning, I attempted to open my eyes, but even the dim light was blinding me, and sparking off a wave of nausea.

Rolling over, I threw up on a cold concrete floor covered with a bit of moldy straw. Sitting up, I held my head in my hands until the room stopped spinning.

Deep breaths, Vittoria. Where am I?

The last thing I remember was arguing with Leo and Carlo and then nothing. Crap! They must have taken me anyway, but why? I thought this was all about helping me get away from my cheating husband.

Keeping my eyes partly lidded, I took note of the small space I was being held in that reeked of blood and fear. *Gross!* I didn't understand why they drugged me except that for some reason, my security team really wanted me away from Romeo.

Were they working for an enemy of the Vitales, and if so, then whom? The only family I knew that had issues in the past was mine, and we'd settled that when my father married me off.

A scent that rung with familiarity punctuated the awful stench of the cow pen I was imprisoned in.

"You're finally awake. How are you doing, princess?" Leo stood at the entrance, but he was different. He'd always reminded me of a wound-up predator, his tendencies barely contained within a taut, muscular body.

Leaning against the iron bars, arms crossed with a smirk on his face, all that tension was gone. He was still a dangerous predator, but not on the prowl. Now he was in his den, relaxed and in complete control.

"What's going on, Leo? Why did you bring me to such a filthy disgusting place?"

His eyes glittered dangerously. "Leonardo to you, princess."

I really hated his arrogant tone.

"Whatever, *Leonardo*!" I enunciated every letter, infusing them with sarcasm.

"Watch the tone, princess, or I may have to muzzle you."

This little battle of wills was getting me nowhere. "Can you please tell me what is going on."

He walked closer to me. "What will you give me if I do?"

Shit! I hoped he wasn't a twisted rapist kind of guy.

"Don't be a pig," snapped a familiar voice. From the far wall, a shadow stepped into the murky light and took on the shape of my father.

"Papa? What are you doing here? What is going on?"

Standing beside Leo, the familiarity finally sank home. The whiff of cologne that had been tickling my senses was the same as the one my father wore. How could I have forgotten? And Leo, he stood the same way, smiled the same way, had the same eyes and chin... No!

"Who is this man?" I stammered, but he didn't have to answer, because in my heart I knew that whoever this man was, he planned on killing me and my father was going to let him.

"Leonardo is your brother, *Colombina*," my father said, smirking at my expression of shock. "Yes, you have a brother."

"You never told me!"

"And why would I? He is my son, my heir, my weapon to wield on the day when the Calogerà family would take back everything they lost to the Vitales. What are you? Just a woman... who has done everything she could to prove to me from a very young age that she cannot be trusted."

My mind raced. I had to get the hell to get out of here and warn Romeo. "Okay, I can understand that," I said with a calmness I didn't feel, "but what am I doing here now? If we're getting out of here, then let's go." I struggled to my feet to show them my willingness to cooperate.

My father and brother smirked at the same time, an old monster and his young reflection. The identical arrogant lift at the corner of their mouths chilled me, a reminder of everything else they might have in common. The fine hairs on my arms stood up. A warning.

"Not so fast, daughter. Leo has informed me of your reluctance to leave your husband." He spat out the last word like it was a bad taste.

"Well, yeah. I didn't know our family was staging a coup. If he'd been honest from the beginning, I would have left him a long time ago. You know I hated the match," I told him, daring an accusatory tone. "If I'd known this was part of your plan, I wouldn't have jumped from my window to escape the wedding."

I didn't mention that I hadn't planned on falling, or how lucky I was that Romeo was there to catch me.

He chuckled. "You were always so rebellious. How do I know this isn't you pretending to be loyal to your family?"

Think... think... "You are right. I have always been rebellious, and I apologize for the trouble that has caused you, Papa, but I was never disloyal, and I'm not now."

My father studied me with the disinterested cruelty of a boy deciding which leg to pull off a bug first, then turned to the man he called my brother. "What do you think, Leonardo? You've been with my daughter for weeks. Do you think she's lying?"

Leo's eyes continued to glitter, his stare so intense that I could all but feel myself pinned by those two pools of blackness. As dangerous as I knew my father to be, I realized this man was worse, not merely ruthless but unhinged.

"So what if she is?" Leo countered. "The family always has use for good liars —" His cold gaze moved over me. "— and well-trained whores. If you think she can be useful to us, I'll keep her and I'll deal with her impertinence in the basement, where all disloyal soldiers go to learn their lesson."

Holy shit snacks! This guy was terrifying, and how I wondered could we be related when we were so different?

"*Scusami*, where have you been all these years, brother?" I kept my tone light and interested, trying to salvage the situation and prove to my father I was on Team Calogerà.

"Calabria. Learning how to lead this family and exterminate its enemies."

"So this is why you spent so much time in Italy, leaving me all alone." I turned a practiced pout on my father, playing the old game between us. "You ignore me to visit my brother? Why did you never bring him home to meet me?"

Leonardo didn't like the forgiving smile my father showed me. Without warning, he sprung at me, gripping my hair so tight I screamed.

"*Basta!*" my father barked. "Let her go, Leonardo! Hurting your sister isn't part of our arrangement."

He gripped my brother's other arm and twisted it behind his back. Leo dropped me and the two of them tussled. I ran past them and out of the pen. I guess they didn't expect me to put up any resistance as there were no guards that I could see. I ran blindly, as desperate to find an exit as the panicked cattle that had once thundered down this self-same chute. Hopefully, I would find a happier ending.

Bang! Bang! Bang! The steady rhythm of someone hitting the metal bars of the stalls with something. If that was Leonardo behind me, and I was pretty sure it was, then he'd won against my father and no one could help me now, but myself.

Don't lose it Vittoria, pretend you're back home. It's all a game.

I removed my shoes and carried them, slinking backwards into the deeper shadows as silent as a cat. The banging stopped; he was probably listening to see what direction I'd gone. I threw one of my shoes as far as I could and heard the soft thud it made when it landed, but did he?

"I've got you now, sister!"

It worked! He went after the shoe and I fled into the blackness, following the wall I found off the killing floor and into a maze of smaller rooms and halls. There was way less light back here all I could do was keep moving and pray I wasn't turned around and heading right back to my brother.

Just when panic began to rise, my hand brushed a padlock holding two ends of a chain together, securing... Yes! A door! I couldn't do anything about the padlock, but there was some slack in the chain. I pried at the unused door and managed to shove it open about six inches, letting in a precious slice of dim moonlight. Was it enough? They say that anything you can get your head through, your body can too. I wiggled my head and one shoulder through when the *bang, bang, bang* started up again.

Crap!

I struggled and pushed and was halfway through when he called to me: "When I catch you, sister, I will teach you to obey with my fists."

Tears poured down my face as I pushed through the last of the resistance, tearing clothing and skin just to get away from him. It was a dark night, with only half a moon in the cloudy sky but after the pitch-black slaughterhouse, I could see enough to run as fast as my feet were willing to go over the pebbled parking lot.

Up ahead, I could see a roadway. I moved towards the side in the tall uncut grass and prayed I didn't step on anything sharp. I slowed down and stayed low. The progress was slow until I heard the sounds of a vehicle from in front of me. Could be a trap. I hid lower and watched as several cars turned off their lights and pulled across the cattle guard and into the tall grass. I listened to the sounds of whispered voices... familiar voices. Could it be? If I was wrong, I'd end up back in there with the monster who called himself my brother.

"Romeo," I whispered into the darkness.

"Vittoria?"

"Oh, thank god!" I stood and ran towards the barely discernable human shapes until one scooped me up in his arms.

"*Principessa*, is it really you?" Romeo cradled me in his arms, and covered my entire head in kisses. Little one, he called me, oh how I missed his terms of endearment, and if we managed to get out of here in one piece, I'd tell him everything, including my stupid childish fantasy of the princess in the tower.

"I'm sorry," I sobbed. "I didn't know. I'm so sorry, Romeo."

"Shh, *Principessa*, it's okay now. I got you. Can you tell me what to expect?"

I quickly filled him in on Leo and my father and the lack of men inside the back of the slaughterhouse, but how I may have ruined any chance of surprising them by escaping and putting everyone's guard up.

"Romeo, please be careful. He's a monster bent on killing all the Vitale men. You're his biggest target, husband."

"Rom, we gotta deal with this before they find out we're here," Tony said.

Romeo's eyes went black and his expression blank. He transformed before my eyes from the loving husband to the cold mafia Don. "Tano, take Vittoria home and guard her with your damn life," he said, passing me into his brother's arms.

"I love you, Romeo, come back to me," I begged as Tano carried me away. The last thing I saw was the men spreading out and disappearing into the fields, silent shadows swallowed up by a silent night.

CHAPTER SEVENTEEN

Romeo

I thought I was dreaming when I heard her whisper come out of the night, but I could tell that my brothers heard it too, and so I dared to answer. "Vittoria?"

"Oh, thank god!" She rose out of the tall grass, limping as she ran as fast as she could right into my arms.

Thank fuck!

She was shaking, terrified, and covered in small cuts and bruises. It had not been an easy escape. Blood stained her clothing in a dozen places and it was all I could do to take a moment and comfort her, when all I could see was red.

But when it was time to hand her over to Tano, I was reluctant to let her out of my arms. I wanted to worship at her injured feet and show her know just how much she meant to me. But now was not the time and I couldn't be with her until I exterminated the enemy.

A small group of us would go through the back and eliminate our enemies in silence. The rest would sneak around and wait for our signal before they opened fire on those posted outside waiting to pick us off, one by one.

Paulo cut off the padlock and pushed the door open. Immediately the stench of old blood assaulted our nostrils. I hated that Vittoria had been stuck here, alone and afraid.

The six of us spread out in groups of three to either side of the building. It was dark and too quiet. Stealthily, we moved forward. I went first while they covered my back, then once they fell in behind me again, I moved forward, and on it went until we made it through the maze of rooms and halls and into a wide-open space.

I heard the sounds of chuckling up ahead and scraping like someone was pulling metal across the concrete. I held up my hand and we moved into position, but before we could advance, there was a loud bang from the opposite side of the structure.

Cazzo!

We moved back into the shadows as seven men raced past us in the direction of the noise, but came back after just a glance and some low muttering. Clearly, they wanted no part of what was happening in that room, but at least some of them found it amusing. As they passed us for a second time, the three of us took them down with our knives, so swift and silent, the last of them was in Hell before he ever knew his friends were dead. One of them was Carlo, and I would be lying if I said I didn't take particular pleasure in carving up the man who had so betrayed my family's trust myself.

Peering around the doorway from where they'd exited. I saw a man beaten and secured with chains. The sounds we'd heard were from a winch pulling the man along the floor. It was Don Calogerà.

His eyes found mine and they were filled with hate.

"You," he sneered. "Why am I not surprised?"

I pressed the button on the winch and Santo was pulled into the air where he dangled looking like food for the machine.

"Your daughter is safe. She managed to outmaneuver that animal you call a son."

His eyes narrowed. "What will you do with me?"

"What I should do is shoot you between the eyes and put you out of your misery. But what I will do is keep you alive until the council decides your fate." Killing one of our own, while not unusual, had to be sanctioned, or else the resulting blood feud could drag in other allies and enemies and destabilize every family's operation. I was within my right to kill the man who had abducted my wife and tried to kill me, but not without the council's blessing. He needed to stand trial before his peers, and given that his unsanctioned vendetta against my family had affected everyone whose shipments Don Calogerà had plundered, I had no doubt his execution would be mine to carry out.

I could see these thoughts echoed in the old man's scheming eyes. "There is an army outside, Vitale," he said. "You'll never get out of here alive. Not unless you let me talk to them."

My men stepped up at once. "Boss —"

I held up my hand indicating silence. I wasn't a fool, there was no way I could trust this guy.

"It looks to me like your men aren't listening to you anymore, Santo. I think I'll take my chances."

I turned to leave.

"You think your men are any more loyal to you, Don Vitale? I've been inside your organization for years. Who is loyal, who isn't... meh, who knows, eh? You haven't brought an army to take me tonight. You've brought mine back-up."

He was trying to screw with my head, and it was working. He was right about one thing, he had infiltrated my organization and with relative ease. When this fiasco was over, that would be the first thing I would fix.

"Paulo, take him down, but keep him restrained. I don't want this piece of shit getting any ideas."

Matteo helped and he was down in seconds. "Let's go. One sound from you, old man, and I'll put a bullet in your head."

We'd been using our blades to keep the advantage of surprise and I wanted to believe that was why we hadn't heard gunfire yet, but my gut told another story. We worked our way back toward the rear entrance. The two we'd left to cover our backs were missing.

"I told you, Vitale," Santo cackled. "Your men are untrustworthy."

I pulled out my phone and texted Massimo. "Get here now, we've been played."

Shots from outside.

"I have your brother, Romeo!" Leo called "I'll trade, your brother for my sister."

Our enemies didn't know Vittoria was already gone, whisked off to safety.

"It's a trick. Don't trade, offer me instead." Don Calogerà insisted.

"As if! This is a perfect opportunity for you to get rescued and shoot my brother," I responded.

My phone vibrated with a message from Vito. His team had gone through to the front first and set themselves up where they could hide amongst the tall grass. Being our sharpshooters, I wanted them to cover us from a distance.

"Boss, it's Vito, we're in position. Say when."

"Run, Leonardo!" Santo shouted.

Paulo rammed the handle of his gun into Santo's face. He crumpled to the ground, blood gushing from his broken nose.

"Now!" I typed.

A rapid exchange of gunfire ensued.

Santo managed to smirk at me from his position on the ground.

"I'd kill you, old man, but I want to see your face when your beloved Leonardo is executed."

Santo's eyes held nothing but malice, but I had no time to spare for that garbage. I left Paulo and Matteo behind to guard him and moved off into the dark, staying in the shadows as I crept around the east side of the building.

I heard a click then. "Got you, Vitale. Move and you die. Drop your gun."

Leo materialized out of the darkness. He was alone, not one for backup, or just so arrogant he figured he didn't need any.

"Doesn't look like you have my brother," I said calmly, setting my gun on the ground.

Leo smirked. "No, but you don't have my sister either, so I guess we're even."

He stepped closer, to kick my gun out of reach and I lunged, wrapping an arm around his neck and pressing down hard on his wind pipe. Leo dropped his weapon to fight me but the safety was off and he got out a shot before he dropped it.

Bang! The world collided as we fell to the ground.

"Let's finish this, Vitale." The bullet had ricocheted off the sheet metal beside us before ripping through Leo's shoulder.

Rolling on top of him, I pressed my thumb into the bullet wound, immobilizing his arm while punching him with my free hand.

I learned a long time ago that hate was a hard thing to kill, as was determination, and the man beneath me had both. Clearly unhinged, crazy didn't even begin to summarize what I saw swimming in the inky depths of his pupils.

He reached up a hand and squeezed my throat, compressing my wind pipe. He was strong and we were evenly matched. I moved my thumb from the hole in his shoulder to pry his fingers off my throat.

Using the distraction as an advantage, Leo surged his body, dislodging me onto the damp grass. He crawled for the gun, but I threw myself on top of him. Gripping his head between my hands, I snapped to the left, severing his spinal column.

"That's for my wife, you son of a bitch!" I picked up the gun and shot him in the back of his head. "And that one's for my brother." I was about to shoot him again when Massimo ran into view with two of our soldiers.

"Are you okay, boss?"

I handed him the gun. "Never better. Where is Vinny?"

"On his way to the house. Tano can look him over when he gets there, but Vinny says he's fine, other than a beat-down."

"Vinny would say that after being beheaded."

"True, but Gio says it too and I'm inclined to believe him."

That was a relief.

"Glad this piece of shit is dead." He toed the dead body. "What about Santo?"

"Mateo and Paulo have him for now. We'll let the council know what's happened here and who's really been behind the disruption to their shipments."

Simo holstered his gun. "So that's it then, it's over."

"Unless some low level *minchione* decides to take a run for the title. But once the old man's dead, Vittoria legally inherits everything. I will ask the council to allow me to merge what is hers with mine, effectively creating ours. And I can't see any reason why they wouldn't."

Simo nodded his head. "Head home, boss. I got this."

"Put the bodies in slaughterhouse and burn it to the ground. I want no trace of Calogerà left. Then take our soldiers and clean out the vipers' nest. They can work for us or die."

I patted him on the shoulder as I passed. "Good work, *fratello*." I left the field of battle anxious to get home to my *regina*, my queen and for the first time in my thirty-seven years, share my deepest feelings with another living person.

CHAPTER EIGHTEEN

Vittoria

Tano kept threatening to tie me to the bed if I didn't sit. The skin on my feet was so torn, they were raw, but with the drugs he'd given me for the pain, I was able to pace while I waited for word from Romeo.

Waking up in that horrible place had been an eye opener for me. Being his wife was the only thing that had saved me in the end, while being the daughter of Santo Calogerà had almost killed me. I shuddered, picturing my brother's level of crazy in his almost reptilian eyes and the words that came from his mouth with a darkness I'm sure rivaled Hell.

How could Romeo's darkness be so different? So needful? Not long after our souls collided in his office, the day where I became familiar with the darkness that lurked inside of him, I'd pined for him, and his knowing touch, his hungry gaze. It was the start of my plan to get his attention. *"O Romeo, Romeo, wherefore art thou Romeo?"*

That seemed like years ago now but the desire for those

things had only multiplied. He came for me, he was willing to die for me.

"*Principessa.*"

I'd been so busy in my head, I'd not heard him enter.

"Oh thank God, you're alright."

His eyes ate me up despite me being a complete mess and in dire need of a shower. He stalked towards me, a man on a mission. I was that mission. Scooping me in his arms, he started for the door.

"Would you look at that," Vinny croaked from the bed where Tano tended him. "Not even sparing a look for his baby brother."

"I know you will heal, *fratello,* and I will be back, but right now I have only one question for you. Where the hell did you hide your phone?"

Vinny winked his least-swollen eye. "Wouldn't you like to know?"

Romeo shook his head and turned away. "I am not in the mood for joking. I have more important things to do right now."

"Sounds like we both have a buzz up the backside," Vinny remarked. "What could possibly be more important than me?"

He was being cheeky and I thought Romeo would blow a gasket but instead his gaze fell on me.

"I need to show my wife how precious she is to me, how almost losing her showed me how much I love her."

"Finally!" Vinny lay back. "Go do that and don't forget to also tell her, she's the best thing that ever happened to you."

"Vincenzo!" Romeo growled.

Vinny managed to smile, even with cracked lips. "Gotcha, *fratello!*"

We left the room to quiet chuckling from Vinny as Tano cussed him about not popping his new stitches.

In our suite, my husband lay me gently on the bed and

undressed me. Then gave me a sponge bath, so as not to hurt my feet. Then he crawled between my legs and sunk his cock into my needy sheath, bathing me in kisses while he slowly made love to me. Each stroke of his cock massaged my inner walls. Each hit behind my cervix sent delicious electric shocks through me.

"Romeo, I have things to tell you that can't wait."

"Shh, *amore,* they can wait just a moment. I need to feel you."

Letting go of my need to share, and allowing him to take the lead, it wasn't long until my first orgasm crested and crashed.

"Romeo!" I cried as my walls spasmed, milking his cock. He joined me, somewhere between earth and the sky with the intensity. It was the first time that my husband loved my body with a sensitivity that made me want to weep.

When he pulled out, he fell onto the mattress, rolling onto his side as he pulled me in tight.

"Tell me, wife, what is so important?"

This was it, the moment to share what I'd been hiding from people my entire life. "I need you. That is what is so important. I need you, Romeo. My entire life I've been pushing people away and being independent, but it's not who I am."

Romeo brushed a stray strand of hair from my face. "I know."

What? How could he possibly?

"I've glimpsed her, when you are at your most vulnerable. The little princess you hide inside where it's safe, *certo?*"

"Yes, for sure. But how? I hid her away when my mother died, along with all of my hopes and dreams. My father began parading me in front of suitors when I was a young teenager. As soon as I became a commodity for that awful man, I locked the princess away in the tower."

A tear rolled down my cheek and Romeo wiped it away.

"Your princess is safe here and I hope you know it. My

regina, my beautiful queen fit for a king. I love you, Vittoria, and your princess brat and every other aspect of you."

Happy tears leaked down my cheeks. "Really?"

"Really."

"I love you, Romeo."

"I love you too, *Principessa*."

THE END

ABOUT ROGUE LONDON

Rogue London is an author of naughty romance designed to awaken your sensual side.

Rogue has a flair for writing about the D/s dynamic and as a true romantic at heart, her books have an HEA.

She also writes as Skylar West.

Like to Read for Free?

Sign up for your exclusive gift First Born Love, by Skylar West.
For more from Rogue, follow her here:
https://www.subscribepage.com/roguelondonnewsletter

https://www.bookbub.com/profile/rogue-london

https://www.facebook.com/authorroguelondon

https://authorroguelondon.com/

https://instagram.com/author_rogue_london

https://www.goodreads.com/author/show/
21620637.Rogue_London

Follow me as with Skylar West on ...

https://twitter.com/SkylarW63773206 tiktok@skylarwest08

ALSO BY ROGUE LONDON

Daddy's Brat Series

Daddy's Sexy Brat

Daddy's Naughty Brat

Daddy's Spoiled Brat

Traveling Brats Series

Daddy's Stowaway

Daddy's Castaway

Daddy's Runaway

Boxed Sets and Anthologies

Billionaires and Brats

Traveling Brats

International Daddies

Multi Author Series Contributions

His Pennsylvania Princess

His Florida Flower

Her North Dakota King

RED HOT ROMANCE

We at Red Hot Romance Publishing would like to thank you for your interest in our books.

If you liked this book (or even if you didn't), we appreciate your taking the time to leave a review on whichever site you purchased it. Reviews provide useful feedback in the form of positive comments and constructive criticism, which allows us to make sure we're providing the content our customers enjoy reading.

To check out more books from Red Hot Romance Publishing, to learn more about our publishing house, or to join our mailing list, please visit our website at:

http://www.redhotromancepublishing.com

Printed in Great Britain
by Amazon